The Diasporan

A Story of Dreams & Deceit

Elliot Chatima and Rumbi Chen

First paperback edition May 2026
Book design by Shabhir
Edited by Elliot Ziwira
ISBN: 978-1-7635933-8-1 (paperback)
ISBN: 978-1-7635933-9-8 (e-book)

Also by Elliot Chatima and Rumbi Chen

The Storm
Landing in Fifteen Minutes
The Land Baron
The gods Above

Acknowledgements

In life there are people whom God has appointed to reveal what he has gifted you at birth and until you meet such people you will not discover that gift. I, hence, treat my invitation by Rumbi Chen to speak at her book launch not as a coincidence or happenstance but a broader plan that God had to reveal the literary gift in me. I am, therefore, eternally indebted, and at the same time grateful to my co-author, Rumbi Chen.

Though our genres were different, we agreed to work together, and *The Diasporan* marks the fifth book we have done together without any incident. The mutual respect and the manner we work together make the nine- hour time difference between Harare and Melbourne nothing to worry about. In a world where people seek personal glory and lifting up their individual names, we have found strength in cooperation.

To my mother Rachel Jima, you departed so early. If one day you get to the balcony of the gods, then, please look down and smile at me. I will feel you, I will receive the message.

Successful outcomes are rarely achieved with individuals working in isolation. Rumbi Chen and I owe a great deal of gratitude to the ever-dedicated Tafadzwa Tamanikwa and Diana Vito for their unwavering support and commitment to reviewing the book page by page, and word by word. To all our beta readers, thank you for your time and valuable feedback. Finally, to our readers: thank you for supporting our work.

Chapter 1

It was a beautiful Wednesday in South Africa's Johannesburg, Freedom Park to be specific. At 4am birds had started chirping, increasing in intensity as different species joined the melodious chorus contestation. The cocks crowed one after another with the sound of the night owl fading as sunrise loomed in the horizon. The big birds disappeared as the sun rose, painting the sky brick orange, penetrating the bushes and awakening animals and humans alike. Only small birds continued tweeting throughout the day: the ones that coexist with humans. These have helped humans realise that it's daytime and time to be productive. Many of these birds depend on feeding on leftover food that humans scatter around each morning. The birds have for long questioned why humans throw away such large quantities of food daily, but language has remained a barrier to communication, precluding them to air their strong grievances.

At 4am, many women and housemaids were awake, preparing children and family for the great and awesome day ahead. Meanwhile, their male counterparts were still in the blankets snoozing the alarm by ten minutes, repeating the act for close to an hour, and in the end, waking up in the last minute to take a shower and leave for work in a huff, hurrying every family member.

For years many have asked if women were able to prepare children for school without yelling. A question that has not been answered, but nobody had bothered to ask for a comment from the women themselves. The matter was better off answered by silence. In life, not everything needed to be put into words; non-verbal communication was better at some point.

The day had started like any other Freedom Park days, as usual people swarmed the streets rushing to work, children going to school and many other activities. The ground frost made waking up difficult for everyone. But like all humans, many eventually make it — a testimony to humans' ability to overcome challenges in life, and a clear demonstration of their determination, patience, tenacity, and steadfastness. Yet again, there were those lazy ones who preferred a little more sleep and a little more slumber in a fashion described in the Bible-- poverty beats them like an armed man.

By mid-morning there was a small crowd of around ten young boys, and not long after that, more boys started emerging from the tin houses like underground creatures, as they seek to escape the heat that was building up in the high temperature attractive sheet metal makeshift houses. Some houses were made of wood; all such houses were referred to as mkuku, a derogatory word for a temporary shelter. The foul smell from movable toilets was difficult to ignore. South Africa, like Russia, had a shitty problem in a literal sense. Many neighbourhoods were set up without underground sewer systems, resulting in messy living conditions. Vehicles came to empty the dotted temporary toilets. Sometimes they took longer to do so.

The boys continued debating various matters to pass time, and by 11am there were about 30 members. They started singing and dancing. A man in a black tinted Ford Ranger pulled up and started talking to the group. As he addressed them; more and more people joined the crowd, typifying the scene in many suburbs with a large number of unemployed youths.

"Fellow South Africans, our country is under attack; we have been invaded by foreigners, especially Zimbabweans. They're the bed bugs that we must squash and spray once and for all. But these bed bugs are stubborn.

"They have taken our jobs. They're stealing from us, murdering innocent women and children. These kwerekweres have even taken our wives, our girls; they're taking everything! They're the reason why we are struggling, and we should eliminate them once and for all. They must be exterminated, because the infestation and contamination they bring is just too much." Zambali fumed as he addressed the people.

"We need to show them that we are serious about getting rid of foreigners out of our country. We want Zimbabweans out of our nation."

Someone from the crowd yelled, "You're right!"

The man who had incited the situation quietly admired it boiling over, as he saw young people taking up matters into their hands. He was pleased that no one had seen him. The youths were about to take over a very tense situation. The lack of capacity to follow the right channels to air grievances meant that this unemployed group only knew one language: violence and use of brute force to beat the 'enemy' into submission.

South Africa had been shaped by violent confrontations from the time of the intolerant Shaka Zulu, a man whose cruelty led to the burying of people alive. Also, cows that had calves at the time of the death of his mother had their bellies cut open. The idea was that the calves were to feel the pain Shaka felt due to the death of his mother. He was fierce in battle and cruel to his subjects and opponents alike.

Owing to his propensity for war and violence, two groups; the Khumalo and the Ngoni people fled Zululand, with the Ngoni settling in the eastern parts of Zambia bordering Malawi, while the Khumalo settled in western Zimbabwe as the Ndebele, claiming the Matabeleland region.

Colonial violence was amplified through the structural and apartheid violent system. The settler state enforced racist policies and programmes through police brutality, forced removals, and systemic inequality, creating a culture of violence. Thus, locals were severely oppressed in their motherland. The system continued to oppress the natives and many were killed on 21 March1960 in what is known as the Sharpeville Massacre.

"Ladies and gentlemen, it's time to demonstrate," One of the frontliners shouted at the top of his voice.

There was hesitation, but after the vigilantes spotted two Zimbabweans; two men and a woman, their hatred grew like a ball of petrol fire from a burst fuel tanker.

One man escaped but soon ran out of luck as the ally he sought refuge in led him to a dead end. The mob caught up with him and picked up stones, and paused, as if waiting for a command from someone. There was division on what to do with the three Zimbabweans.

"Let's spare their lives but embarrass them," someone in the crowd shouted.

Judging from the murmurings, it was not easy to determine what each one was saying.

"Embarrassment is not enough, these people want a stronger signal if they are to go back to their countries. We should use terror; they have to be terrified of living in South Africa. Only death can deliver the message we seek to put across," a woman protested.

A boy, barely ten, shouted, "Kill him."

He threw a stone at Nelson, the Zimbabwean man. The stone fell short, but it became a turning point. The mob followed suit.

Nelson closed his eyes. He was "no longer" at the scene. His mind was somewhere else. He was in a forest back home in Zimbabwe. He was playing a game with birds like he used to do. He had trained eagles, and this time the massive birds were flying. Scratching his clothes, from time to time, the birds increased in number. They attacked him, but he was relishing the sight and resisted opening his eyes.

Nelson was in another world but in reality, all the scratching that he was feeling were stones being hurled at him remorselessly. He had switched off to turn the deadly moment into a mind game to avoid dwelling on the inevitable end he was about to face, aware that he was in the shadow of death.

In a flash, he saw his mother calling him, imploring him to be strong and to always be watchful as he was going to a country of endless opportunity and danger in equal measure. These were the words his mother had told him before he left Harare on his maiden trip; a one-way ticket journey to South Africa, or a boarding pass to heaven or hell depending on one's fortune.

Nelson was bleeding from the head. He fell to the ground, motionless, attempting to deceive the people into believing that he was unconscious. Unfortunately, one woman aimed a stone at his head but missed. She was shaking with fear, yet the desire to show that even women could be decisive, was getting the better of her. The mob laughed mockingly.

At that point, she turned and picked a bigger stone, moved closer to Nelson's "lifeless" body, and standing over the prostrate man, like a goddess of doom, she stared at him, trembling, afraid of what she was about to become—a murderer, a female killer.

No one had killed anyone in her family judging by the stories narrated about the clan right from the great-grandfather to the present generation, yet there she was, a woman out to prove that she was as capable as men—of causing harm, of killing. She did not have a clear personal interest in the matter, but her involvement was to be documented in the history books yet to be written. She fancied the possible fame that would come with it; it was irresistible, it was appealing, and it was worth dying for.

Legs akimbo,, chest protruding, betraying firmly erect breasts, she was such a woman; the kind that would make a great wife. She had all the feather beddings that a man could ask for in a woman: a rounded ass and hips that did not lie; yet there she was, joining a xenophobic war against foreigners. It was difficult to judge what she was exactly planning to do, but that was not important. She held Nelson's life in her hands.

"You Zimbabweans are hard nuts to crack. You have invaded out space here in South Africa; why can't you just go home and build your country and leave us here to enjoy our own?" Lindiwe demanded, holding a big visibly heavy stone. . It was just a matter of time before she dropped it.

It was clear to all that she did not have what it took to throw or drop the stone and end Nelson's life.

Nelson turned and gestured to Lindiwe.

"Please spare my life and I will leave the country at once; you will never see me again. Please my sister, don't kill me," Nelson begged.

Lindiwe's tears flowed down her cheeks, depositing some in her dimples, with the rest continuing effortlessly like Mutarazi Falls in the scenic Eastern Highlands of Zimbabwe. She was emotional. A mother's instinct kicked in and she regretted taking part. She decided to save Nelson's life.

She lowered the hand holding the stone slowly, and just as the pebble touched ground, but still in her hand, a boy yelled.

"I told you guys, this work is not for women; women are weak, frail, afraid, and made only to give comfort to men!

"They are good for bearing children, nursing them and cooking for the family. They must be left at home to bath and look good preparing themselves for men when they come back from work. They should be ready to give us pleasure," the boy insulted Lindiwe.

Still holding on to the stone, she was not perturbed. She was firm in her resolve and wanted to be accredited for stopping the senseless killings that had rocked the country.

So, she was quiet till the boy shouted, "Move over baby mama, you are too weak for this; next time stay home, in fact, go home to the kitchen where you belong!"

Lindiwe summoned all her strength and lifted the stone. In a single motion of her hand, she crushed Nelson's skull, killing him instantly. The mob continued throwing stones, signalling the start of xenophobic attacks in Freedom Park, Johannesburg, South Africa, shedding innocent blood. All foreigners retreated to Eldorado Park where they were protected by mostly people of colour, who had guns to fend off the menacing angry mob.

The other two Zimbabweans, a man and a woman, were forced to watch.

Tinei was dragged in front of everyone, and, in a court like session, a muscular man was holding what looked like a gavel, with a T-shirt wrapped around the head to mimic a judicial wig, the type worn by judges in many former British colonies. The "judge" was seated ready to pass judgment.

"I find you Tinei, a Zimbabwean man, AKA Kwerekwere, guilty of entering South Africa, taking our jobs, our girls, and our freedoms. You're hereby sentenced to death by burning or stoning.

"Since we have already witnessed death by stoning, I hereby sentence you to death by burning with petrol till fire saps all the blood in your veins," the "judge" said hitting the gavel.

He looked at Tinei and asked. "Do you have anything to say?"

He made little effort to contain the impatience and his eagerness to see the verdict actioned.

Tinei gazed at the kangaroo court judge.

"My lord, the judgment is too heavy for your servant. May you please reconsider? Your servant has three children, a wife and a mother who is blind whom he is taking care of back in Zimbabwe. Your servant will leave your great country at once and will never come back. Please, have mercy on your servant, for he has a valid work permit and was staying in your country lawfully," Tinei begged.

There was silence in the "courtroom". The judge was faced with a complex matter, but in the end, he ruled that Tinei was still guilty for taking away jobs. He hit the gavel again and Tinei raised his hand.

The street judge was getting impatient. The street witnesses were waiting impatiently.

"Speak," the judge demanded.

Tinei cleared his throat and began: "My Lord, even in death there is dignity; please allow your servant to pray to the Christian God to accept his spirit."

"Very well", the judge said, suppressing tears, and acting strong lest he be called a weak man.

Tinei knelt down, prayed and sang. Even those in the kangaroo courtroom sang along to the beautiful songs that he hummed. When he broke down mid-prayer the people felt sorry for him.

Tinei lifted his gaze to the judge, looking him in the eyes for a moment. Then, someone came from behind and announced, "It is time."

Tinei was taken away, hands tied.

On the horizon, a convoy of police cars was approaching at high speed after a broadcast of the kangaroo court was beamed. Tinei beamed with hope and his heart was raced. He wanted to be saved, but he had connected to his creator and was ready to face any situation, yet the lingering thought of his blind mother kept nagging him. It was the only thing holding him back. Regarding his wife, he was sure that she was going to do her best. With their inherited property, they were going to manage.

The police cars were inching closer, sirens screaming. The crowd was dispersing one by one, but the closer the police were, the more thrilling it became. The mob was determined to carry out the death sentence.

The guy who was holding a cigarette lighter left. Tinei had a tyre hung around his neck, filled with petrol, and as the police details shouted and fired warning shots in the air, a ball of fire raced past them towards Tinei. The angry fire engulfed him and he screamed with excruciating agony. The police rushed to save him but it was too late. He had sustained high degree burns on his chest, neck and face.

He called out his mother but it was all in vain.

When the police left, Tinei and Noel's bodies were collected. The mob regrouped and dragged Zandile into the street to fulfill their desire to send terror and fear into the hearts of all foreigners who were listening and watching.

Zandile was brought before the angry mob. A South African woman came running and pleaded with the mob to spare her life as she was her housemaid and a good citizen with the requisite papers.

One woman stepped forward and charged. "Look here, we do not want to be accused of partiality. We have just killed two Zimbabwean men here through stoning and burning. This woman is not an exception.

"The men here will defile her. She will live but will tell her story to everyone as a key witness. She must narrate the stoning and burning of Zimbabweans and the story of how she was violated by uncountable men."

At that point a man arrived and introduced himself as Zandile's husband. He pleaded for mercy and asked if it was okay for him die in her place. This touched the women there, and they almost gave in, but that was not part of the agreement.

James was a fine-looking man. Hands bound; he was dragged and forced to watch his wife slapped in front of him. Zandile was stripped naked, and the first man came and tried to fondle and caress her, much to the frustration of those waiting for their turn.

"Fuck the bitch or step aside, man. We're already waiting here with our guns ready," one horny man yelled.

Another one stepped up from the crowd, undid his zipper and raped Zandile—no caressing, no foreplay, no protection—just raw lust and grave hate. He was inside her for almost five minutes, pumping and shaking her. She screamed with pain, but the more she screamed, the more the women cheered. Countless men took turns to molest her until she felt dizzy, her screams of agony, bleeding heart, broken spirit and soul unheeded. She was brutally violated while her husband watched.

Three young girls aged twelve, fourteen and sixteen were brought to the scene where their mother was being molested. They too were raped countless times, screaming and kicking in both pain and anguish.

As if that were not enough, a man hauled four tyres, necklace Zandile and her children and drenched them in petrol but before they were set on fire James shouted, "Stop!"

"Please put me there as well. I want to die with my family. I have seen enough and I cannot live after what I have seen."

Sbu walked to the centre, looked James in the eye and spoke. "Look, man, we are here to set an example, so that when our story is told, there will be eyewitnesses to support it. We want a testimony from someone who witnessed the event. . Such a testimony is powerful, hey. So, please don't take this personally. We are still brothers; Zimbabweans and South Africans. All we want are a few examples. You and your family will be used for a higher purpose."

James looked at him in disbelief.

"You are clearly a weak man, raping an innocent woman and her children. What kind of a man are you?"

James was trying to provoke them into killing him as well.

At that point Sbu motioned and James' lastborn daughter was set ablaze. She screamed, "Daddy, please save me; save my life daddy. Please daddy, don't let me die!"

There was silence. Then, another child and another. And it came down to his wife.

Tears streaming down her cheeks, Zandile looked at James shaking her head. She screamed so loudly that her voice was only drowned by the gust of fire that roared and burnt her to death. James witnessed it all—painfully, silently.

Sbu looked at the mob.

"I bet you all are thinking we are overdoing it. We are still by far the most loving people in the world, but we want to free South Africa for South Africans.

"Now we have our witness; an eyewitness who will tell the story with so much passion. He will spread the fear we seek to instil in all Zimbabweans and other nationals: Mozambicans, Malawians, and Nigerians. He is now our ambassador, who shall speak on our behalf."

A police vehicle was approaching, and in a last-minute bid to cover up, they stoned James and ran away. Fortunately, when the police arrived James was still alive. He grabbed the petrol container and poured fuel on himself. He moved to his now deceased wife, and boom, he was up in flames.

The family of five was gone; killed in a senseless xenophobic attack. The principles of the liberation struggle to free Africa from colonial clutches were up in smoke. The likes of Nelson Mandela, Oliver Tambo, Samora Machel, Robert Mugabe, Julius Nyerere, Kenneth Kaunda, Kwame Nkrumah, among many other gallant sons and daughters, who fought to free Africa, were turning in their graves.

Meanwhile, in another unrelated event, it is payday at a farm in Mpumalanga. Approximately two hundred employees are gathered to receive their salaries. They had been waiting since 8am. At exactly 12-midday the farm manager emerged.

"Good afternoon, everyone. We decided to pay you in kind—with grapes since we have run out of cash. I am sure you can find your way into the city and sell the grapes. Those willing to do so, please move this side," the farm manager said.

There was commotion as the farm workers, mainly foreigners, the majority of whom Zimbabweans, started singing and chanting. The farm security guards were called, and they promptly opened fire, killing ten workers and seriously wounding five others. .

The farm workers quickly took the bodies of the severely wounded into the pig feed warehouse.

"Boss what shall we do? We have ten dead bodies and five workers in a terrible condition. What shall we do with these people?" the farm security officer asked shivering, having not killed anyone in his life.

The manager looked at him as if assessing his loyalty he motioned to the pigsty.

"Sir, I don't think it's a-", the security officer wanted to protest.

"You are paid to follow orders not to think," the manager interjected.

And so it was, ten bodies were thrown into the pigsty to be immediately devoured by pigs. Then, unbelievably, the manager ordered that the five wounded be thrown into the same place. Desperate screams cut across the afternoon sky as they were mauled by the pigs alive, too weak to defend themselves.

For the next ten minutes there were loud screams from the doomed pigsty. When two of the wounded workers attempted to escape, the manager opened fire, instantly rendering them pig food, with neither remorse nor emotion.

Chapter 2

About a kilometre from the scene where Tinei was killed, a Zimbabwean woman was spotted by a different vigilante mob locking herself into a tin sheet house. The angry crowd drenched tyres in petrol and burnt them on either side of the shelter, igniting unbearable heat.

The woman took hold of one of her children, and threw her to safety, as the heat intensified. She flung the second one, and by the time she pushed the third out the fire had engulfed the entire house, burning her instantly. The gas tank in the house exploded, spreading the fire in all directions, making saving her an uphill task. To make matters worse, there was no one in the vicinity willing to save her.

The children screamed in unbearable anguish, unable to take in the loss of their mother in such a horrendous way. She was all they had. They knew no one else in South Africa. The vigilante mob was elated to have three young witnesses whom they trusted to preach the news and spread the much-needed fear among the Makwerekwere, a derogatory moniker for Zimbabweans living in South Africa.

Later that day, the three girls were taken to a local hospital near Soweto. After registration and as they waited to be examined by a doctor, a team of men wearing military fatigues stormed the hospital.

"If you know that you are a foreigner, step aside. All foreigners out; we can do this nice and easy, in a peaceful manner, or we can use force. If you know you are a foreigner, leave this hospital," the team leader yelled.

In the meantime, the girls were limping along from burns suffered from the fire. It was such a sad sight to behold, but nobody cared.

The fated woman was later identified as Lizzy in a video that went viral on social media platforms. Her brother Nathan recognised her children. Fear and grief consumed him, sadness of the heart gripped him, and he trembled. Even in the company of friends, who did their best to comfort him, he couldn't bear the loss of his sister and what befell his nieces. It was just too much for him. No words could comfort him.

The following day, he suffered a stroke. Nathan played the video over and over again, and as he did so, his blood pressure shot up. Three days later, he died in his sleep, leaving a wife and two children, in addition to his late sister's three children.

It was a load too heavy to carry for a widow in a hostile foreign country, but life had to go on. There was no hope in Zimbabwe; no jobs, no potable water, no dreams. Everything was dead as people lived from hand to mouth; and hospitals were death traps. Nobody dared to think about going back to Zimbabwe.

Nathan was married to Lorraine, a loving and supportive woman. She was appreciated by many, but when Nathan died, things got hard and she had to survive. One night, she called Loliwe, one of the deceased Lizzy's daughters, now 15 years old.

"Loliwe, I am sure you are old enough to see what is happening here. We lost your mother, and my husband is no longer here to look after us; you need to look for a job and start doing something with your hands," Lorraine explained.

"Yes auntie, I am grateful for your good heart. Life has been tough for you. It's not easy for you to look after five children single-handedly," Loliwe replied.

"See now, that's why I love you. You understand and perceive things that even older people find difficult to . I like your maturity," Lorraine responded, patting Loliwe on the back.

"So, auntie what options do we have. I am so excited to be able to assist you with the bills," Loliwe replied almost immediately.

"My dear, have you ever seen a penis? That small thing can give you the life you want if you know how to handle it well. All you need to do is learn how to play with it. There are men willing to pay whatever price just to get it inside the right person," Lorraine remarked, looking at Loliwe to gauge her response.

Loliwe laughed out loud, narrowing her face. "Tell me you are joking, right?" she quipped.

Lorraine's face had completely changed.

"Tomorrow you will be going for training on how to do a body massage. You will be massaging mainly foreign men. After that, you will learn how to amuse your clients and offer them bliss. That's where the money is; one client can give you up to R2 500, and that's cool money to take home daily as a tip.

"Later, you will serve three men per day, making at least R7 500 per day. You can be your own boss, imagine! What do you say to that?" Lorraine explained, exposing a smirk on her face.

It became clear to Loliwe that she was being introduced to prostitution at a higher level. That night she thought about her sisters and how she was going to look after them if she were to refuse the job offered. They were probably going to be chased away.

"Good morning auntie. I have had time to think about the matter. I am going to do it my way, she said hesitantly but resolutely. "I will go the lesbian route, since it's safer for me. I have made up my mind.

Lorraine looked at her in disbelief. She wondered how a 15-year-old girl could make such a choice on sexual orientation, but it wasn't important at the moment.

"I hear you baby girl. That's your call, so long you bring food on the table," she replied.

Loliwe prepared for work immediately. When she showed up at number 19B3 Bree Street at Mama Bliss Massage Parlour, she was welcomed by the lady of the house herself. Mama Bliss was a streetwise elderly woman with hot searching eyes and dressed elegantly.

"Wow! Look at that! Mama Bliss exclaimed, examining Loliwe the way a cattle merchant does at a heifer offered for sale.

"How are you my dear? I have heard great things about you. What an honour for you to come and work here!"

Loliwe was stunned. Her first impression of Mama Bliss was that of a graceful, kind and patient woman, who made her feel like somebody, which made her conscious of her self-worth.

"Here, have a cup of coffee and some biscuits, while we chat. We have a lot of catching up to do," Mama Bliss said, revealing a set of dimples on her old wrinkled face, which, despite the passage of time, was still beautiful, though in an exotic way.

"Mama Bliss, the services provided were top-notch..., and I bet this is your latest inventory! Is she the virgin you were talking about? Shame, I saw what happened to her mother! But with a perfect body like that, she has nothing to fear at all. Her body is exactly what she needs to conquer the world," one old white man yapped as he handed R3 000 to Mama Bliss as a tip.

Loliwe was seated there trying to understand everything that was being said. She had been marketed and men were already looking forward to sleeping with her. She was overwhelmed that she was seen as inventory not human being. It was the most disturbing thing ever said of her. She wished her mother was still alive, but that was in the past. In reality, her dearest mummy was dead.

Later, she was shown around the parlour, and introduced to the other girls who worked there. Of the 10 massage rooms at the premises, only three were free, while the rest were occupied.

Moans of ecstasy could be heard from at least three adjacent rooms, which made Loliwe sick. She was scared, wondering what would become of her if started sleeping with men—different men for that matter. What kind of example would she set? But morality and survival are a delicate balance. In a moment of need, it is easier to justify any action.

Loliwe was introduced to Sandra, the trainer. Sandra was to handhold and train her for three weeks, after which she would be given dummy clients to serve as the final interview.

"Good afternoon Loliwe. What a nice name!" Sandra greeted her.

"Good afternoon to you. How is work? Do you think I can do this job my sister?" Loliwe asked, displaying the fear in her eyes.

Sandra comforted her offering a glass of classic mojito without alcohol: "Here please; take a sip as we talk."

At 3pm a client walked in and Sandra grabbed him by the tie. She cat walked ahead of him and once clear of the reception area the client slapped her ass. She occasionally stopped to express how she felt. This continued till they were in the consultation room. Sandra stripped to her panties and bra. She started massaging the client while Loliwe watched.

Sandra was on fire—electrically and gracefully teasing her client. She was in charge. She was standing over him as he ripped off her bra, exposing her tender big boobs. She mounted him and he slipped his erect manhood into her sending both of them into screams of pleasure in one smooth motion. Sandra worked wonders on him as he twitched and jerked in delirium.

Her head reeling, Loliwe watched intently, all the while fighting the urge to join in a threesome. It could be a great idea! She contemplated. After quite some time of sexual torture, she rushed to the bathroom and held onto the wall behind the toilet seat and cistern—panting as her lungs fought for air. She hadn't experienced such nudity and 'sin' before. She could feel a jelly-like fluid flowing down her thighs, confusing her all the more.

As abruptly as it started, the initiation was over.

The following day, Loliwe had her first client. As a virgin, she hit the jackpot, with the lucky client tipping her R35 000 for deflowering her. Initiated into sex, she could only look ahead. Life had just begun. She had dreams—huge dreams. She would send money back home. She managed to acquire passports for her sisters and applied for their student visas. Back home in Zimbabwe, she built houses and drilled boreholes. She was known as a banker based in South Africa. She was a well-respected member of the family. At her peak she would serve at least four men per day. During weekends she worked in a brothel boat in Cape Town selling sex and ancillary services to at least three men daily for two days and earning US$500 from each client. Hence, a good weekend would earn her US$3 000 plus tips. She even obtained an investor's VISA and opened her own massage parlour.

Chapter 3

As the xenophobic attacks raged on in South Africa, many people were making decisions to leave Zimbabwe for the diaspora, a clear indication of how desperate the situation in the country was.

Meanwhile, in the mountainous countryside of Nyanga in Manicaland Province, a gang of school leavers were playing a game of Crazy 8, which is their daily routine. Unable to secure employment since leaving school, they involuntarily started gambling, drinking illicit brews, like Tumbwa and abusing drugs like Crystal methamphetamine (Crystal meth), commonly known as mutoriro or guka, BronCleer and other substances to while away time and come to terms with their miserable lives.

The five boys were all Advanced-Level graduates, with three of them having studied sciences, but failed to secure funding to further their studies. One studied commercial subjects; and the other one, a razor-sharp nerd, having passed with 14 points. Again, money was the issue. Once beaming with confidence and having very high hopes in life, the boys were slowly sinking into despair.

"Boys, we are getting old playing cards. Why don't we make a plan?" Farai said. There was silence as if no one heard him. There was an unspoken subject. Nobody wanted to confront this elephant in the room. The fear was not finding a solution, which would further push them into depression. So, until there was a clear direction or plan, the matter remained taboo.

"My man, what are you talking about?" Gabriel gathered the courage to ask. Farai looked at him with a knowing but inquisitive eye. He knew that they had to have a new dialogue. He admired birds of the air as they flew past, focusing on them a while as if their flying formation were a solution to their quandary. Lost in his own thoughts, Farai was unconscious of his friends' glare at him.

"Fatso, tell us; what's on your mind? Have you come up with a way out of this miserable life. Tell us man, we are thrilled already," e Simon inquired.

Farai looked at the rest of the team to gauge the mood and determine if what he was to say would be accepted.

"Guys we have a situation here. Our occupation here will get us nowhere. We should get out of here fast," he said.

"Cut the soft soap, man. Why are you beating about the bush man? Just say it and let the decision on the way forward be ours," Gabriel declared.

"Guys, I have been pondering; maybe we should try it out in South Africa, the land of gold. I am told there are great opportunities there, hey! What's your take?" Farai threw the ball back in their court.

"Are you out of your fucking mind, man? People are being killed daily in that God forsake land of xenophobes. Just yesterday, a video of an entire Zimbabwean family being burnt to death went viral on social media, and you want us to go there? If you want to die, I can kill you here right now. At least your relatives will have the honour of giving you a proper body viewing," Simon responded in a voice tinged with both anger and irritation.

His fury was so visible that one could touch it.

"Farai has done nothing wrong. Let's allow him to put his plan on the table. What's on your mind, man?" Gabriel asked softly.

"Guys we can cross the Limpopo River into South Africa and look for jobs there. We will lie low, exploring opportunities in farming areas. I know of someone working there, so we can make a plan," Farai explained.

"Okay; what you are saying is that we skip the border, evading Zimbabwean police and plunge into the raging waters of the Limpopo infested by hungry crocodiles and swim across? And all the while deal with the police and military officials with a helicopter hovering above us?" Simon asked dejectedly.

"What's the difference, my guy? Isn't it better than remaining stuck here and die of depression? As for me, being hit by a bullet fired from a helicopter or wherever else, or mauled by crocodiles is a mark of greatness," Farai said soberly.

"I can't wait here and die slowly from alcohol and drugs. I need a fresh start."

Assuming the leadership role, Farai declared: "So, we leave tonight gentlemen. There is no time. Go home and gather what you can. We will tell our parents when we are on our way and switch off our phones. We will only talk to them upon arrival."

The die was cast. At 6:30pm four of the boys met at their rendezvous, and the other one was nowhere to be seen. After waiting for an hour, they decided to send Simon to check him out. But after waiting for a further 30 minutes, the remaining three guys decided to leave without them. They hitch-hiked to Harare in a Mazda 3 being driven by a stern looking young man in his late 20s or early 30s. The journey took about two and a half hours.

Having no business in Harare, they hitch-hiked to Masvingo, then to Ngundu, and finally, to the pick-up point. When they arrived about 30 people were already waiting to cross into South Africa. Farai, Gabriel and Takudzwa had made it.

As reality sank in, the boys, who were becoming men, felt the exuberant feeling of adventure evaporating. It was now a matter of life and death. Nine hours of travel from Harare to Beitbridge was as exciting as it was promising, but it was no guarantee to a better life. One had to fight for it, survive and overcome hurdles. The greatest test lay ahead, yet there were no assurances of hitting the jackpot across the Limpopo after overcoming all that was to come. Nonetheless, the odds were better than in the motherland.

Jorum, their contact person, received them among scores of other people who arrived in different buses from across the country, having braved their way to the Zimbabwean border town of Beitbridge. There was an air of suspense as the fortune seekers gathered around to listen to Jorum and his crew of 10 men.

"Listen everyone; this journey requires a facilitation fee of US$30 per person. You also require R100 for the police and soldiers across the river if you make it," Jorum explained.

"There are deep waters in the Limpopo, therefore, cooperation is of utmost importance. One misstep you will drown or be swept away by the strong current, since it has been raining lately and the river is flooded."

Jorum took frantic glances at his watch, his eyes darting around for possible danger.

"Considering the crocodiles in the Limpopo River, the likelihood is that some of you may not make it, although we have assisted many people across without incidence," Jorum said.

A bushy narrow deserted way led to the crossing points along the Limpopo River. The journey was the most treacherous and punishing for Zimbabweans seeking a better life in South Africa. The river was flooded after several consecutive weeks of constant outpouring with tributaries pouring their burden upstream.

The river roared from a distance as the border jumpers moved in silence. The lead team moved with care and skill. Some guys were ahead and used South African lines to communicate the status of the route. Then the moment of reckoning came. About halfway across the crocodile infested river, a man, probably a father or husband, was charged at by one of the hungry reptiles, giving him no chance to even say goodbye to his loved ones. The girl in his company desperately broke free to try to rescue him, but was immediately swept away but the strong tide. This sent shivers up the spines of the seekers of fortune in foreign lands, who had to silently take it all in, for neither speech nor scream was allowed.

Like in the animal kingdom, there was no time to mourn the dead. One needed to keep moving.

Guided by the gods of fortune and their ancestors, Farai, Gabriel and Takudzwa were among those who successfully crossed into South Africa. They found their way to Mpumalanga where they got menial jobs.

Chapter 4

The first session of the newly elected South African Parliament promised to be fired up. Many issues of national interest, including security, were to be tabled and debated. There was also a state-of-the-nation address by the president coming up, a Finance Bill to be amended, a supplementary budget to be implemented without approval by parliament, raising temperatures among opposition parties. Before midday, the president received three phone calls from his African counterparts—no ordinary calls by any measure.

"Hello," President Cecil Namakosa answered the first call.

The phone was on loudspeaker and was being recorded as is national security protocol. It had come through a secure line—an official line allocated to the president.

"Hello my friend. This is President Ikechukwu Tinabi from Nigeria. How are things over there Mr President?" he asked casually.

There was a brief moment of silence then President Namakosa came alive.

"Good morning, Mr President. How is Nigeria?" he asked in a faint voice, betraying his fear of what was to come.

"Well, the Nigerian inland and pretty much everywhere else are doing very well. It is my people living in your country that I am concerned about," he responded.

"I am aware of the disturbances in my country, but to say all Nigerians are well, save for the ones in my country, is an insult Mr, President, sir, , especially given the mass abductions of defenceless young girls in schools, whom you have failed to protect year after year," President Namakosa replied tersely and unapologetically.

His frankness was probably either motivated by the distance between them or preoccupation with something else.

"We shouldn't be fighting, in my view. I seek only the safety of my people on your land—African land and our motherland—who are being chased like mangy dogs, killed and molested in the streets. They're being treated like animals under your government's watch," President Tinabi cut in.

His tone was rather deliberate; not loud, not too low, just right. It was difficult to ascertain his temper or mood.

"Mr President, our nation may be having its own challenges, but we are certainly handling the matter. We are on top of the situation," President Namakosa replied.

"Mr President, we have always accommodated your companies here in Nigeria, offered them licenses to operate freely, and allowed them to repatriate their profits to your country. It is, therefore, difficult to imagine why your government fail to stop the attack on my people," President Tinabi responded containing the urge to shout, although his voice betrayed his anger and frustration the way a season debater does.

A moment of silence followed as the two counterparts traded measured words to express their positions without overstepping diplomatic boundaries.

"Mr President, you have my word. We will do everything possible to ensure the safety of your people and other African nationals in South Africa," President Namakosa broke the ice.

"You may do as you please, Mr President, but in the meantime, I have instructed our embassy to make travel arrangements for all Nigerians who wish to leave your great nation. I cannot sit and watch while my people are being killed and having their businesses destroyed. That is my final word Mr President," President Tinabi said.

"Well, you are doing your job as the President of Nigeria, and that's expectable. We shall cooperate and deliver on your request. I, however, would like to assure you that this incident is not a reflection of our great relationship." President Namakosa said.

"Mr President, may I remind you that this is the third time my people have been hunted down like dogs and have had their throats slit open like chickens, yet no arrests were made and no one has been held responsible. Let my people go, Mr President or at least allow me to offer safe passage to those willing to leave," President Tinabi said in a firm authoritative voice.

In the end, the logistics were worked out, and 14 planes provided to evacuate Nigerians who wanted to go back home to safety. There was a wide media coverage in what turned out to be South Africa's most embarrassing moment.

Later on, President Kufazvinei Matambudziko, affectionately known as President Kufazvinei or simply President Kufa, of Zimbabwe called. He was in his office at State House in Harare when the call was put through. The discussion centred on bilateral trade, cooperation within the Southern African Development Community (SADC) region on issues of peace and stability. Finally, President Kufazvinei asked directly.

"My dear brother, Mr President, is the situation getting any better, considering the disturbing scenes I have seen? Are you winning in dealing with the widespread violence?"

President Kufazvinei's tone was gentle as he was aware of the thorny nature of undocumented migrants in South Africa, especially that the largest number was attributed to Zimbabweans.

"Mr President, you and I know the burdens we carry in the wake of continued flow of undocumented migrants from many countries, including Zimbabwe. It's a problem we need to deal with, not only here in South Africa but in your country as well. I believe Zimbabweans, under your capable leadership, should play a leading role in dealing with economic, healthcare and educational issues in Zimbabwe. As South Africa, we remain ready to assist you to resolve these matters," the President of South Africa said.

"You are right Your Excellence, the removal of some of the illegal sanctions imposed on our country by the West has resulted in an improved economic outlook. We have started investing in the refurbishment and modernisation of our healthcare system. On behalf of the Zimbabwean people, I am grateful to your government for accommodating our citizens," President Kufazvinei remarked.

The last call came from the President of Malawi, who in summary, sent 28 buses to pick up Malawians willing to go home. The whole morning was ruined for President Namakosa. Soon after the calls, the South African Intelligence Organisation apprised him on the security situation in the country. He walked into the briefing, fully aware that the xenophobic attacks were going to dominate the discussions of the day. However, there was something else; something more damaging.

South Africa's intelligence briefings are largely known to focus on possible threats like economic instability caused by either internal or external forces or a combination of both, with immediate or long-term implications. They also deal with cybercrime, transnational crime, and state security, coordinated by the National Intelligence Coordinating Committee (NICOC) through documents like the National Intelligence Estimate (NIE).

Recent developments include the General Intelligence Laws Amendment Bill (GILAB) (GILAB), aimed at modernising intelligence gathering, addressing bulk interception, and enhancing oversight, reflecting shifts after the Zondo Commission's findings on state capture. Key priorities involve protecting South Africans, territorial integrity, the economy, and cyberspace, with increased public participation encouraged.

The National Intelligence Estimate (NIE) 2019–2024 is an evidence-based assessment of threats and opportunities, covering economic, territorial, state authority, well-being, and global threats.

The National Security Strategy (NSS) 2024, endorsed by Cabinet, provides a framework for national security efforts, focusing on protecting citizens, sovereignty, economy, cyberspace, environment, and culture.

The "chairman" of South Africa's intelligence briefing structure isn't a single person, but involves leaders like the Political Head in the Presidency and the Inspector-General of Intelligence. Key oversight sits with Parliament's Joint Standing Committee on Intelligence (JSCI), overseeing bodies like the State Security Agency (SSA) and Defense Intelligence.

On that particular day, the meeting started at 08:45, which was 15 minutes later than the usual time. The reports were shared and after exchanging good mornings, the president motioned for the chair to begin.

"Good morning, Mr President, sir. May I ask the esteemed First Lady to excuse us as is standard protocol?" the chair said, his voice pleasant, firm and respectful. The president had asked his wife to walk him to the office but they proceeded into the meeting.

The First Lady jovially raised a fist to the chair, sending the whole presidential boardroom into rapturous laughter. Nobody took it seriously since she meant no harm. She was such a pleasant character, whom they affectionately called Mama.

"Mr President, the honourable ministers of Security, Foreign Affairs and Home Affairs, generals of our esteemed armed forces and intelligence unit here present, ladies and gentlemen," the chair saluted the house before proceeding. There was a sense of urgency in his voice.

"Today, we are seized with a matter threatening the territorial integrity and economic independence of our great nation. The xenophobic attacks on foreign nationals had sent a worrying signal to investors and expatriate professionals alike. We believe this culture of violence on innocent people should be addressed immediately," he continued.

"Mr Chairman, what is the damage so far? Do we have an assessment of the damage; and what control strategies are in place at the moment?" The president asked, taking notes. Adjusting his tie, he stood up briefly before sitting on the edge of his exotic leather executive chair.

The chairman looked at the Foreign Affairs Minister, Lilian Zulu, who had been called in to explain how the matter had to be handled.

"Mr President," the Foreign Affairs Minister started, "we are working with Home Affairs to determine the most appropriate response.

"We have scheduled a media briefing this afternoon at 2pm and I am optimistic that the Police would have arrested some suspects and covered ground to show we are in control," Minister Zulu remarked.

"Minister, I want a realistic plan soon after the meeting, we will lose credibility. The stock market is in red, global custodians are demanding answers, and development partners are worried. The United Nations is assessing the situation and our adversaries are already calling it a genocide. We cannot allow the trajectory to go on like that," the President said unaware that he was shouting at the top of his voice.

"We take note of that Your Excellence. We will have a comprehensive response to the matters being raised in the 2pm press briefing," the minister said.

"Your Excellence, we have received Intel that a number of suspects have been apprehended. We believe this will give us ammunition in the press briefing later today," the Home Affairs Minister remarked, betraying his uneasiness, perhaps due to the mounting pressure for justice.

"Mr President, we have received information that the President of the United States has expressed his intention to boycott the G20 meeting to be held here next year. He made reference to what he called brazen human rights abuses at a grand scale," The chair of the intelligence community said.

There was silence before General Macmillan reacted: "We should stand our ground, Your Excellence. Senseless killings of unimaginable proportions have been recorded in their backyard. We cannot allow the politicisation of the xenophobic attacks. We should, therefore, show strength, not weakness. If we exhibit weakness, then we are doomed."

"Which events are you basing on, General? The chair asked.

"Mr Chairman, may I refer you to the Black Lives Matter hashtag, a clear example of how not to forget the historical savagery of slavery? No one can lecture us on an internal matter we are managing," General Macmillan responded almost immediately.

"Very well, we have received a letter from our ambassador in the US saying there are considerations to withdraw our nation from the AGOA scheme.

AGOA (African Growth and Opportunity Act) is a United States trade law enacted in 2000 that grants eligible sub-Saharan African countries duty-free access to American markets for thousands of products, aiming to boost economic growth, good governance, and US-Africa trade relations. The programme excludes countries such as Zimbabwe, though the country has made tremendous efforts to thaw the frosty relations between Harare and Washington. While it has significantly increased African exports and fostered development, the programme was set to officially expire on September 30, 2025, with ongoing efforts to re-authorise or restructure it, creating uncertainty for African economies before the date of expiry.

The programme offers duty-free access, providing tariff-free entry into the US for over 1800 products, covering both textiles and non-textiles. This is aimed to support economic growth, create jobs, promote market-based reforms, and strengthen US-Africa ties. Eligibility is based on criteria like democratic governance, rule of law, and protection of human rights, with 32 countries currently designated. Among its impacts is that it facilitated nearly US$500 billion in exports from Africa to the US. Between 2002 and 2022, supporting sectors like textiles, agriculture, and motor vehicle manufacturing.

The chairman took time to explain the programme and its devastating implications if the threats were taken seriously. It was clear that the xenophobic attacks constituted or were being viewed as constituting human rights abuses, a critical precondition for a country to benefit from the programme. The president needed no lecture on the impact of AGOA withdrawal. He knew that some industries would scale down operations or close down.

The chairman briefly scanned the room, before continuing, in a calmer voice.

"Our last item on the agenda is the proposed economic sanctions on our exports and visit to the US by certain government officials and the recalling of our ambassador.

"The ambassador has been given 24 hours to leave the country as he has been labelled a persona non grata, which is an embarrassment to our country, "the chairman remarked.

He was showing signs of fatigue from sleepless nights and being overwhelmed by matters that needed to be resolved. It was such a long week on both the domestic and diplomatic fronts.

In the afternoon, a press conference was held, with the Home Affairs Minister, chief of police and Foreign Affairs Minister present. All the big international and local media were present. The Home Affairs Minister was the first to speak.

"Good afternoon, ladies and gentlemen. We are gathered here at a sad time—a moment that does not bring pride to our nation. But we want to let you know that we will overcome. We will thwart these acts of banditry in their infancy in which hooligans masquerade as concerned citizens against foreigners.

"The long arm of the law will catch up with those found on the wrong side of our statutes. As we speak, 32 suspects are in police custody and are assisting with investigations, which are ongoing nationally," he said.

An army of hands shot up as journalists sought clarity.

"Good afternoon, Minister. I am Lisa from the Voice of Africa. Honourable Minister, in view of your long history of alleged corruption, fraud, abuse of office, murder, and human trafficking, would you consider yourself the right person to handle this matter? One journalist asked, visibly shaking.

The minister looked at her, initially intent on dealing harshly with her, thought better of it, and toned down. He looked at her again and smiled.

"My dear, anyone can be accused of crime; that's the normal nature of life. However, if you insist that I was convicted, then that's a totally different matter altogether. Tell me, do you recall any case in which I was found guilty and convicted by a court of law? The minister responded with a smirk on his face. He was enjoying how this was unfolding, aware that the reporter had been defeated.

"Perhaps you are smart in your dealings. But the fact that these allegations were raised against you renders your integrity questionable," she retorted.

The minister took out his tablet and typed her name. There were accusations that she was in love with her boss. She was said to have been bad mouthed at work and initially dismissed before being later found innocent.

"So, shall I also conclude that you were in love with your boss and all the accusations being levelled against you? See, you and I have a lot in common: our work puts us directly in harm's way," he remarked mischievously.

Three other journalists were given chances to ask.

The first one was from the Daily News International.

"Minister, is there a timeline on the prosecution of the accused people; and what compensation is being granted to the victims of xenophobic violence—both survivors and the deceased?" he asked.

"Our duty is arresting and taking them to court to face charges. The courts will determine the timelines in terms of the law, but generally, the matter is of public interest, and I want to believe that cases will be tried within reasonable time to ensure that justice is delivered without fear or favour," the minister responded.

"Minister, is it true that some of the people fronting these violent acts are members of political parties currying favour with the electorate?" Joel from the Guru News asked.

Well, it's difficult to comment on an ongoing investigation; we will, however, follow the leads and advise accordingly. We are going to have press briefings every top of the hour to give you updates on new developments," the minister concluded.

Chapter 5

The sunset brings a serene atmosphere to many people as birds chirp around their nests dangling from treetops and inside holes drilled into trunks. Their varied melodious tunes reminds one of the way stock birds fly in a diamond formation on their annual migration from Africa to Australia.

Along the mighty Zambezi River, different nocturnal animals come alive, including snakes, hippos and hyenas. Day animals, such as waterbucks also frequent these parts in search of water, oblivious of lions lying in wait to pounce on them at the slightest opportunity.

The delicate circle of life hangs in balance, any destruction leading to imbalance. When animals devour each other in broad daylight, one may struggle to see the hand of the God in the savage and raw nature of hunting in the jungle. That is how it is meant to be, though.

Humans also frequent the Zambezi River for fishing and sunset cruises.

On a Monday morning, as all that played out, Nancy boarded a bus from Harare to the mighty Victoria Falls. The falls were always known to the Lozi and Tonga peoples, who called it the Ngonye Falls and the Shungu Namutitima (boiling water), respectively. The Shungu Namutitima recognised that turbulence and the great intensity of the Zambezi River as it flows from the Quadripoint. The Lunaya people called it Dhubu Dhubu, a derivative name from the bubbling sound that the water makes as it hits the rocks at the bottom of the waterfall.

Basing on this, David Livingston's purported discovery of the Victoria Falls clearly defeats common sense. The man only gave it a new name, in honour of Queen Victoria, and popularised it. It has always been known as Mosi oa Tunya (the smoke that thunders), by the local people.

Indigenous nomenclature does not only depict the physical aspects of the Victoria Falls, but reflects their spiritual significance as well. They signify life, peace, abundance and essence of the gods; hence connecting deeply with the indigenous people and reminding them of its sacredness. God, the Creator, whom they called Musikavanhu, lived in their midst, with the river speaking of his presence and creation; his provision of water becoming the greatest assurance that he was with them. Water provided them with game, fish, and tourism opportunities, creating livelihoods for them across generations.

The Victoria Falls, one of the Seven Wonders of the World, offers many activities that a visitor can become a part of; from bungee jumping at the Victoria Falls Bridge, water rafting, canoeing, crocodile caging, game drives and helicopter aerial views of the entire falls.

Well, Nancy was a chef hired to cook for both local and international tourists. She enjoyed her work, but the responsibilities at home were taking a toll on her, hence the need for a well-paying job. She had gone four months without a salary and hope was fading away. The country's economy was getting worse.

The first child in a family of nine children, Nancy ended her education at Ordinary-Level. She had to free the limited resources at home for her siblings. Soon after her exams, she did a course in culinary arts, and had to immediately find work to augment the family's income.

Nancy's trip by bus took fifteen hours, instead of the usual twelve. The Bulawayo-Victoria Falls Road was damaged beyond repair. The road brought so much shame and embarrassment to the nation. In one viral incident, tourists used the large potholes on the road for photo shooting to portray Zimbabwe's neglected roads.

Nancy was one of the first people to get into the "Horizon Cruise", one of the hired boats used for sunset tours. The Horizon was a beautiful boat, measuring 160ft long, 48ft wide and weighing 230 tonnes. It is the largest luxury cruise boat patrolling the waters of the Zambezi River. It is big enough to take large parties of up to two hundred and thirty people on day trips for an unforgettable magic holiday cruise enmeshed in the gentle breeze with the sunset providing a backdrop to an unforgettable scenery. As has been the case since time immemorial, the sun hugged the waters, producing an awesome image that would remain logged to memory. From a distance, the falls could be seen spraying the sky as described by the "Sun, Steel and Spray" dreamer, who did not live long enough to see it.

Cecil John Rhodes, the imperialist godfather, had a dream to connect Zambia and Zimbabwe through constructing what became one of the most spectacular works of engineering assembled by the French engineer, Metcalf. Around the boat, were other smaller ones with a number ranging from 10 to 50 depending on size. Each time a boat passed there were cheers as members screamed and waved at each other.

From time-to-time, hippos would expose their heads then submerge into the water. Sightings of hippos increased as the boat got closer to riverbanks.

Nancy was seated on the top deck with a team of twenty visitors she was guiding after. They had booked for the boat cruise as part of their package. The initial idea was to get a smaller boat which meant little to no interaction with different people from many countries.

On the menu were barbeque, roasted nuts, sandwiches and many other delicacies. Beer, wine and whisky were on the house. Nancy was far away, her mind in faraway lands. She was thinking of how to leave Zimbabwe; a motherland once touted as the breadbasket of Africa, but now home to the poorest of the globe. Millions were facing starvation and living on hand-outs from different humanitarian institutions. Unemployment was high, inflation hit the sky and the currency changed every nine to 15 months, also, domestic and external debts had reached unsustainable levels and international lenders stopped all forms of loans and assistance. The situation was dire.

Amid all that, Nancy knew she needed to do something.

While scrolling on her phone, she received a WhatsApp message from Sharon Magunje, one of her friends. They were in the same class and both did not proceed to Advanced-Level.

"Hey sweetheart! It's been a long time. How are you doing?" Sharon remarked.

"Mm-mm, who is it? I am lost, hey," Nancy responded with a love emoji.

"Kkkk, that's what happens when one has made it in life. They forget their relatives and friends. It's your girl Sharon, remember, from high school? I am so offended, hey!" Sharon replied with a sad emoji.

Immediately, three dots appeared on Sharon's phone as Nancy started typing.

"OMG I am so embarrassed girl. How have you been? I have been looking for your number, hey! So good to reconnect with you once again," Nancy responded, adding an emoji of a happy person and another throwing love kisses.

"Girl, we need to talk, hey! I am fed up of living in this hell," Sharon retorted.

This time she put an emoji of a red-faced angry man. One would have expected the face of a woman but it did not matter;

affirmative action was least of her worries. It was clear that she was, indeed, sad and angry at the same time.

"You are a reader of minds, my girl," Nancy replied with an emoji suggesting, 'Bring it on'.

"Baby girl, we should talk United Kingdom, hey. Let's go and do care work and nursing. This madness isn't getting us anywhere; we are getting old by the day. And we have nothing to show for it," Sharon said, exposing both anger and desire at the same time.

"Girl, I am down. Whatever it is, count me in, hey," Nancy confided.

"For starters, we should enrol for the Red Cross course and get six months experience. I will send you the list of what needs to be done, but you can do all these without ever raising a finger. The desperation in this country can get you anything you desire, girl." Sharon responded almost immediately, and then sent an emoji indicating association with people in higher places.

"Sharon you never cease to amaze me. It's about time you PMD. How is this going to work girl?" Nancy inquired.

"PMD; what's that girl?" Sharon asked.

"Put me down, hey!" Nancy clarified.

"Girl, we should meet like yesterday. You owe me US$100 for school fees and US$150 for practical lessons and certificate. I have your papers. Can we meet tomorrow? I hope you have a passport?" Sharon said inquisitively.

"Girl, what are you saying? Please don't get me excited. And, yes, I have a passport," Nancy replied.

"We should meet. There is no time. We need to apply for jobs and get sponsorships. You better come to my place tomorrow morning. We should be done by the end of the day. It'' quiet a process, hey!" Sharon said.

Soon after, Nancy called someone, and when she was done, she looked sad.

"Hey, what the matter with you; are you alright, ma'am?" one of the tourists asked with concern.

Nancy was quiet for some time, reading everyone's mind. She knew she had to be smart and play her game well without exposing herself. She lowered her head, trying to exhibit sadness and it worked perfectly. She cupped her head with both hands, slowly wiping the tears that had flooded her eyes. It was a trick she learnt from her ex-boyfriend who worked in the intelligence department. It was a coping mechanism.

"My mother is very sick; I am told she has been rushed to hospital," Nancy said.

She spoke in a horse and faint voice. Her sadness was pronounced as she burst into tears. It was such a wonder how she managed to do it effortlessly. Her boyfriend, Tavaviwa, was the champion behind it all. According to the concept of induced sorrow, one needed only to concentrate on a moment where they were treated unfairly and relive the pain of that moment. The idea is to think through it over and over again, until the whole scenario dominates the mind. If it takes longer, then a personal current pain point should be focused on. That works wonders and if sibling rivalry is added, it would definitely get one really sad.

So, it was for Nancy. She was deep in thought about her mum.

The group of tourists they were catering for whispered something among themselves, and when they were done, one of them asked.

"Nancy, do you have your passport or ID with you? Did you travel with it here?" he started.

Nancy did not respond immediately.

"Nancy?" The man asked again.

She snapped out of her deep thoughts and raised her head as if she had not heard the man the first time.

"Do you have your passport with you, or your ID?" he asked again, this time showing deep concern. His colleagues shook their heads, expressing pity and sympathy at the same time.

Nancy looked at him, then downcast, uninterested in the assistance at hand. She want would come up following her act. She expected to be dismissed immediately to give her ample time to travel during the night. For a moment, she gathered courage. It was too late to change the story.

"I appreciate your help, but we are not allowed to interact and exchange financial favours with clients. We have a strict code of conduct, which doesn't allow me to either look right or left," Nancy said firmly and with finality, instilling both awe and respect in the tourists.

She stood up and took three shots of vodka before serving chilly chicken wings.

"Nancy, I spoke to your manager and she agreed that we can help. We bought an air ticket for you. You are on Fast Jet, which means you should depart tomorrow", the tourist added. He was literally begging Nancy to accept their gesture of goodwill.

Nancy was quiet, her mood difficult to read. She walked straight to her manager and before she could speak, the representative of the tourists stood in the middle.

"What is this boss; you know how much this job means to me? I have siblings and parents to take care of. How do you approve of such a transaction?" Nancy said, her voice betraying neither anger nor calm disposition.

Though not shouting, she wasn't composed.

Tabeth, her manager, was taken aback. She had been looking for an honest employee like Nancy in a long time, yet she was standing right in front of her, encouraging her to leave for better opportunities.

"Nancy, your mom is not well and you need to be in Harare to be with the rest of the family to decide what to do together. If anything happens, you will never be able to forgive yourself," Tabeth explained, her eyes locked in Nancy's.

Nancy looked at her for a moment like a boxer sizing up an opponent. As usual, it was difficult to judge what was going on in her mind. Finally, she broke down in tears and went on her knees to thank Tabeth and the tourists for their kindness.

"Here", said the benevolent tourist handing her US\$350 to use when she got to Harare. Nancy gladly accepted the money, a smirk on her face threatening to ruin everything, although she decisively thwarted it.

When the boat docked, the rest of the team went to Boma to be consumed in traditional dances, African cuisine and cultural interactions, while Nancy headed to her room to prepare for her early morning departure. As soon as she got to the hotel she switched on the television and turned the volume to maximum, screaming singing and dancing excitedly. Almost immediately, a WhatsApp alert flashed

"Hey girl! This is Jeff, the guy who handed you the money earlier today. How are you? How is mum doing?"

Nancy panicked, unsure what to do or say. She had to keep the lie alive. She had called home and told them everything. As it turned out, Jeff had called home to check on Nancy's mother.

"Thank you so much, Jeff. That was very kind of you. How is she?" Nancy said, trying very hard not to sound alarmed.

There was a moment of silence. Nancy, being a clever girl that she was, knew that Jeff was up to something, but she didn't know what it was. She didn't have to wait longer to find out, though.

The three dots on the WhatsApp application were flashing again, this time taking longer than before. They flashed and stopped and Nancy was not sure what to expect anymore. She put the phone down and decided to take a shower.

When she came back, there were three messages. When she read them, she was stunned.

"Nancy, I don't know much about you, but I like you. I like the way you carry yourself." Jeff had put an appropriate emoji to go with the message.

Nancy was dumbfounded, unsure how to respond, but help was not very far away. Sharon took 13 seconds to type, "Play hard to get but don't be rude. You never know."

Nancy was soon engaged on WhatsApp with Jeff.

"Thank you so much for your kind words, Jeff. You realise, though, that I am at work, and can be in serious trouble for speaking to clients in this manner, but I appreciate your message," Nancy responded almost immediately.

"I hear you. How about meeting after this trip when you are not at work and we see how things go?" Jeff said.

"You don't take no for an answer, do you?" Nancy remarked attaching an appropriate emoji.

"Should I take that for 'yes'?" Jeff asked, encouraged.

"It's a big maybe," Nancy replied, neither dismissing nor confirming anything, but enough to keep a man interested. She was trying to avoid a situation where Jeff would come to her room and use her like she had seen happening to other girls. Yet the more she played hard to get, the more Jeff felt challenged and wanted to continue pursuing her.

Jeff had hoped to get a quick fix and get laid that night. When he was rebuffed, he felt his ego bruised but not battered. He developed a genuine interest in Nancy and was now willing to do what took to spend some time with her, regardless of the schooling he was up to.

She resumed her WhatsApp chat with Sharon.

"Hey girl! I am sorry for taking too long to respond. I was busy with Jeff. He is asking me for a date, imagine," Nancy said.

"Baby girl, I thought you were asleep, hey. That was quiet a show you put up there; you still have it in you," Sharon responded with an excited emoji.

"So, tell me, what's the plan? What time are you getting here? We have plans, you know," Sharon said.

"I am told the plane lands at the Robert Gabriel Mugabe International Airport at 11:15am. I don't even know how I am going to get home. My friend, this is better be worth it, because I have told so many lies. I got an air ticket and some spending money from clients on the basis of a cooked-up story," Nancy wrote.

"*Haaa makanyanya vasikana* (you are too forward, girl). How did you pull this one? I think the debate and public speaking skills you had at school are coming in handy," Sharon commented with an emoji of a woman holding a wine glass.

The following day, an airport shuttle bus was ready to pick up passengers at the newly refurbished Victoria Falls International Airport. Nestled about 18 kilometres from the town of Victoria Falls, the airport receive air traffic directly from Harare, Bulawayo, Cape Town, Johannesburg, and Kruger National Park, among other international airports

The Victoria Falls has a number of hotels, among them, the Elephant Hills, which has a capacity of more than 600 rooms, including conference rooms. Across the Zambezi are international hotels such as Avani and Radissons. On the Zimbabwean side, there are a number of campsites and world class lodges ranging from US$50 to US$250 per night depending on one's taste and affordability.

In Victoria Falls, a delicate balance and coexistence exist between humans and animals. Warthogs, baboons, elephants and hippos frequently visit the town. The human-animal conflict is often with elephants. Across the Zambezi, some hotels were constructed on the elephants' corridor and each rainy season they roam around paths they once used as crossing places.

Chapter 6

Nancy checked out of the hotel in a hurry. She almost missed her plane. She sat at the back of the quantum bus inscribed "Shear Water", behind whose wheel was Mr Mlilo Dube, a middle-aged man of middle height with vast driving experience. He was making announcements but Nancy was not listening. She was going through her WhatsApp messages with Jeff, who was up to something again.

"Good morning, beautiful. Hope you slept well. You are always on my mind," he dropped a message at 05:22am.

Another came at 05:45: "Hey, girl; please wake up and make preparations, lest you miss your flight." And yet another at 05:59am: "Hey girl; please wake up. You will miss your flight."

As she went through the messages, Nancy couldn't help blushing. She hadn't felt that way in a long time. She wondered if she was falling for Jeff or he had simply touched a nerve that hadn't been aroused in a long time.

Unable to hold on to the excitement, Nancy forwarded the messages from Jeff to Sharon. Her friend was quiet for three minutes, then the three dots started dancing in a Mexican wave again, not pro max but light.

"Wow! This guy is serious. Please keep him interested; you never know," Sharon replied.

"Baby girl, don't raise your hopes too high," Nancy laughed through an emoji.

The driver spotted painted dogs and slowed down to let them cross. He explained that painted dogs stay deeper in the forest but from time to time follow kudus, especially when they migrate during the reproductive season.

The bus sped-off, meandering through the expansive road, before slowing down to give way to a herd of elephants one of which had a young calf. Elephants are protective of their young ones, and if they sense danger, they form a protective wall around their offspring.

One bull elephant attempted a mock charge but realised that the bus was out of reach and retreated. A mock charge is when the eyes are wide open, but when they are pinned backwards it spells trouble.

The Victoria Falls International Airport loomed on the horizon; a beauty in the middle of the jungle. On reflection, it would have been interesting to hear what animals had to say about this human creation; but did it matter?

"Ladies and gentlemen, may I have your attention please? We have arrived at the mighty Victoria Falls International Airport. Please make sure you have your passport handy, and remember to collect all your bags. Thank you for visiting the Victoria Falls. Travel safely, and please call again!" the driver announced and immediately opened the door.

The driver offloaded all the bags and as the passengers disembarked, they were greeted by therapeutic traditional music from a local group at the entrance. Nancy remembered that she had not responded to Jeff and had to do so, although she wasn't sure if she would be able to do so.

"Hey boy, did you sleep well?" she sent the message accompanied by a cowboy emoji.

It did not take Jeff a minute to respond. She appeared to have been expecting the response.

Nancy went through the check-in process and got her boarding pass. As she crossed into the departure lounge, someone behind her whispered, "Hey girl, can I talk to you?"

Nancy turned and realised that it was a random man looking for her number.

"Good morning, Mr, sure we can talk. What is it about? How can I help you?" Nancy asked politely.

The guy moved closer and looked around to see if there was no one listening, then whispered:

"Well, I saw you from a distance and I admired your structure. You are such a wonderfully made woman, and I was wondering if we could have a chat? I want to get to know you better. By the way, my name is Noel," he stammered.

"It's great to meet you, Noel. Are you looking to marry or you want someone to play with? Let's be clear from the onset," Nancy asked.

Noel was caught off-guard; he didn't see it coming. It hurt like three strong punches in the gut.

"Wow, you really know how to put things across, don't you? Anyway, I want a life partner, depending on how we connect," Noel replied.

"You are struggling to say you want to play with me. The thing is, I have had one boyfriend and had sex three times all my life, so I should say, I am a low mileage car," Nancy stated the facts "My current rate for playing is US$1 300 out of town per weekend, out of the country outings will set you off US$3 500 week. A once off sexual encounter is US$450 per session of three hours, with the drinks on me.

Also, there is a US$350 on boarding fee and US$200 starter pack. How is that?" Nancy put her cards on the table looking Noel straight in the eyes.

Noel was embarrassed and felt challenged at the same time. Feeling challenged, he reached for his wallet and pulled out US$550 in crisp $50 dollar bills as payment for on boarding and starter pack. Nancy accepted the money and asked for Noel's number.

At that point, a boarding call was announced and Noel was visibly shaken. He had allowed ego and unbridled desire to take over reason. That was the last time he saw Nancy. He had hoped that she would call but she never did.

Nancy strode graciously to seat 6A. Noel was tempted to ask her to sit next to him as the plane was not full, but being the gentleman that he played, he dismissed the urge to do so. The doors were closed and soon the captain was on the microphone.

"Good morning, ladies and gentlemen, I am your captain, Linda Makuti, and with me here is first officer Simon Tanga. We shall be taking off shortly for Harare. Our expected travel time will be fifty-five minutes, and we shall be cruising at an altitude of twenty thousand feet. Weather: pretty clear skies, temperature at 26 °C. We expect a smooth ride. However, we may expect some turbulences as we approach the Robert Gabriel Mugabe International Airport," the captain announced.

In the meantime, the plane was taxing to the runway while one of the airhostesses was demonstrating safety features, and after getting clearance from the air traffic control tower, the 55seater Ambrea aircraft sped off and in exactly 38 seconds it was off the ground. Nancy looked over from the window, as the falls faded in the distance with the town of Victoria Falls further off in a breathtaking view. The jungle beneath was such an awesome sight from above.

Inside, Nancy was conflicted. She enjoyed the pleasure of travelling by plane for the first time, yet guilty conscience lingered on. She lied to win people's compassion and shamelessly accepted money from a stranger on the promise of sexual favours. Of course, the guy was showing off, but was she justified to get the money—the whole US$550 of it? But above all, the one thought that continued lingering over her mind was that she was about to become a Diasporan. She wondered how life was going to be. For some strange reason, there was no fear of obstacles ahead, but the fact that she was about to change her life for good and living in new environment, was mind mindboggling. She was afraid of the unknown.

The airhostess came with a yellow box with an assortment of food and water. Nancy tucked it all away to eat later on.

There was a beep and the captain came on the mic again: "Ladies and gentlemen, we are not in Chegutu and soon we shall begin our descent. We expect to land in fifteen minutes, clear skies are expected."

The announcement was followed by another beep. The airhostess followed up with announcements about sitting upright, folding al tray tables, opening window blinds, and fastening of seat belts.

Nancy wore a sneer as the plane approached the VACI for landing. The view of Greater Harare, specifically Southlea Park and Chitungwiza, was great. She was not sure whether to thank God for the experience or just let it be. While she was still pondering, the jumbo landed safely, much to the applause of the passengers.

Chapter 7

Nancy went through arrival formalities at the newly facelifted Robert Gabriel Mugabe International airport. The airport was still receiving manicure and pedicure but the view was already beginning to look modern. The domestic terminal was temporarily connected with the international one by a long recently erected corridor. There were benches on the sides to allow travellers and those accompanying them to seat while waiting for their flights or check-in time.

The aerial view of the airport had changed from that of a tiny rusty establishment to a polished upmarket facility capable of receiving international delegates. It had been President Kufazvinei's dream to have the public transport system revamped. He had targeted international airports in his strategic national development plan, where tourism had been identified as a pillar for anchoring economic growth.

There was a high-pitched beep with small speakers placed, perhaps, too high and a poor sound drowning the words being said. One had to carefully listen.

A WhatsApp message came in.

It was from Sharon: "Hey girl, where are you? Have you landed yet? I have 101 things to talk to you about."

Nancy replied: "Hold on baby girl. We have touched down beautiful. I will be out soon waiting for my luggage."

"Wow, you sound like you have been flying for years," Sharon responded almost immediately.

While Nancy was typing, a WhatsApp call came in. It was Jeff. She wasn't sure if she was going to manage a conversation with him while in a public space.

"Hi Jeff. I have just landed at the Robert Gabriel Mugabe International Airport. May you please allow me to go through arrival formalities; I will call you back as soon as I am done?" Nancy answered before disconnecting the call.

She looked at her phone briefly. There were three messages from Sharon but before she could respond to them there was an incoming call. She looked at it for some time; caught between answering and ignoring it. She eventually decided to answer.

"Hello, good morning. This is Nancy speaking; how can I help?" she said

The caller was quiet for some time, then, in a peculiar, accent answered. "How are you my sister? I hope you travelled well. This is Mlilo Dube. I gave you a lift to the airport in our shuttle; do you remember me?"

"Of course, I remember you. How can I forget you? I hope everything is okay, my brother."

"Yes, my sister. There is only one small issue. I have a little diary with no name; the handwriting seems to be too perfect to be that of a man. The diary contains a number of issues that are rather intimate. Could it be yours?" he said.

Nancy was quiet for a moment, thinking. Her diary contained very intimate issues. She journaled every event in her life. There were moments such as sex with her neighbour, sex exploits with tourists in the moonlight, among other embarrassing issues, and closely guarded family secrets.

"My brother, please read one page of what you think is the most embarrassing issue, then I will tell you if the diary is mine or not," Nancy said after a brief hesitation.

"Well, you may want to brace yourself for this one," Mlilo Dube said, clearing his throat.

"Today, I met a man of my dreams; tall handsome, quiet, wealthy. He walks with grace, a small faded smile on his lips, a chest firm and crisp, his hand firm and warm. His kiss, slow and passionate, his attention undivided, his grip strong like a lion's paw yet gentle like a dove. His reading of my rhythm, accurate and on point, never rushing ahead nor legging behind; his mannerisms gentle, his whisper to my ears seeking approval to delight me reveals his gentle yet respectful charm. He moves with grace, stroking my velvet. Looking intently into my eyes, he tells me how beautiful I am. He kisses me with a purpose; he turns me with grace; he holds me with a reassuring firm grip; and lifts me with the strength of an elephant, holding me firmly in his arms and gently delighting me till I am spent. I cry out with pleasure, I cry out with never ending bliss of lovemaking. I want to be held in his arms every day. I want this strength of a man to dominate me and defend me, guard me and protect me."

When Mlilo was done reading, Nancy rushed to the bathroom. The reading of the script reminded her of Michael Paradzai. It was vivid, as if she was reliving the moment. It was fresh in her mind, though it had been six months previously. She had to change, hence she rushed to the bathroom, and soon after closing the door, she went into spasms--panting as if she was gasping for breath, then she realised that she was wet. The thought of Michael made her come instantly.

"Ma'am, are you still there?" Mlilo shouted. He cut the call after hearing some weird sounds from the other end. Five minutes later, he called again.

"Yes, the diary is mine. May you please keep it for me? Alternatively, you may send it through FedEx at once. I will send you the money required for the services. Thank you very much in advance, my brother," Nancy pleaded.

"Ma'am, I am glad I have found the owner of the diary. However, I have one challenge: my wife saw it and got inspired. She wants me to put to practice some of the things that you encountered.

"I need some notes on what I should do to manage the kind of performance that some of the men listed in your book achieved with you," He said.

Nancy was quiet for a few seconds, then responded: "Tell your wife that what's written in the diary is work of fiction; tell her that I am a writer."

"I am afraid she is an enlightened woman; she knows that everything there is based on experience. Well, I will send the diary and call you later when done with my shuttle services," he finally said before cutting the phone.

"Good morning, ladies and gentlemen; may I have your attention please? May passengers from Victoria Falls please pick-up your baggage from the carousel. Please verify your baggage before you leave the airport," a lady's voice announced over the top notch public address system. The luggage carousel span and rolled, as it hissed and spat bags continuously fed from a conveyor belt.

Nancy waited for her bag, which seemed to take forever to come. She waited for about thirty minutes, scanning the bags from their flight. She soon realised that no more luggage was coming. She had paid little attention to the bag that had been circling around the carousel—similar to hers, yet it wasn't. Then as if something happened in her brain to trigger action, it immediately dawned on her that her bag must have been switched, a common occurrence on larger long-haul planes, though rare among domestic airlines due to the smaller number of passengers. Nancy had dashed to the toilet soon after arrival, which could have been the time her bag was switched. The next three hours were traumatising for her.

Nancy turned to an airport marshal.

"Good morning, sir; I don't seem to see my bag. I was on a flight from Victoria Falls," she explained. She didn't realise that she was shaking. She must have been stunned by the development; first flight, and boom, a crisis.

The marshal looked at her intently. It wasn't clear whether he was admiring her curvy body—an hourglass-like shape with a raised chest and erect breasts or not. Nancy was beautiful, but the many struggles she encountered in life had given her little time to contemplate.

"Sir, I am talking to you; I have lost my—," Nancy repeated. The marshal snapped as if in a spasm of some sort: "Ma'am, I heard you, please follow me."

They walked through the gates to the mishandled baggage. There was a small desk in a corner, but there was no one to attend to them.

"Ma'am, this is where you will be attended to. If you face any challenges, please let me know. I will be around to assist. Perhaps, you may want to take my number in case you are stuck," the marshal said reassuringly.

"Thank you. I am cool; if I need anything, I will certainly look for you," Nancy replied.

"I am only trying to help, ma'am. I know it can be frustrating to lose one's bag. I just hope you will find it," the marshal said.

As he walked away, a lady walked into the mishandled baggage section. Already, an hour and a half had gone.

"How can I help you?" The woman asked pulling some forms. She was looking the other way oblivious of Nancy's misfortune. To her, it was just another day in the office, another mishandled baggage, and no big deal. When she was done, she handed over the form to Nancy to fill in.

The form was long and winding, requiring the usual background information; colour and type of the bag, and three distinct items in it. Nancy filled in the paperwork, and when the bag left on the baggage carousel was brought to the office, it was discovered that it belonged to one Jonathan Waffle, possibly a tourist

The standard practice was that they would try to locate the person using information captured during ticketing.

"Ma'am, we have taken down your details. We shall try to contact the owner of the bag we have at hand since you say it's similar. We believe that based on the information provided, the bag may have been switched. We shall contact you as soon as we have information regarding your bag. In the meantime, you may go home," the lady explained. Though she started off indifferently, she softened and served Nancy diligently.

Chapter 8

Nomsa Chikonye was navigating the brutal winter that ravaged South Africa with temperatures reaching minus three degrees Celsius. Her husband Thomas Samson Chikonye, affectionately known as TSC, a bricklayer by profession, had accompanied her to the Southern African country.

The couple had gone through a series of challenges. They had been looking forward to having children. However, Nomsa had had three operations owing to an infection in the intestines, which required immediate removal of the affected part. Later on, she had a bladder infection, also requiring an operation. Then, came three miscarriages in succession. Yet, in all that, the two managed to persevere, finding strength in the Lord to soldier on. The role played by the local church in strengthening and supporting the family was never to be taken for granted.

Looking back at all the troubles they faced over the years, the couple looked content.

"Honey, nature is calling. Let me go to the ladies," Nomsa said.

"I am not sure about that, my dear. You are due anytime, and this could be a baby coming," Thomas said.

"I know how excited you are about the baby that's about to come, but I think you are overdoing it. Slow down babe boy. The baby isn't coming anytime soon," Nomsa playfully said, caressing Thomas' chin.

"Well, I can't wait to hold that baby in my arms. You, of all the people, should understand by eagerness," Thomas said, fondling Nomsa's belly from behind.

She turned gently towards her husband, a smile appearing on her lips, revealing the two dimples that amplified her beauty.

"I must say we have built this family brick by brick and layer by layer, and many materials were tested and found unsuitable as the foundation of our marriage," Nomsa said thoughtfully.

"My dear, you speak with profound wisdom. You are a better builder than I am. My love for you is iron clad— firmly rooted. I am your number one supporter and fan," Thomas replied excitedly.

The pending delivery of the baby after more than ten years of marriage had brought hope, excitement and anxiety to the couple. Nomsa was aware of the emotional trauma that her husband was going through. The scan had revealed that the baby was a boy, yet despite that, Thomas, perhaps like his namesake from the twelve disciples, doubted it. By the eighth month he had asked his wife to go through four scans to get confirmation that the child was, indeed, a boy and that he was in good health. He had doctors checking up on his wife every week from the nineth week of the pregnancy.

As the lovebirds exchanged pleasantries, a call came through from Nomsa's mother.

"Hello mommy. How are you doing?"

I am well. We are just counting down the days now. It can happen any day," Nomsa replied.

"You should walk uphill; it will help prepare the path for the baby. The dilation process will be faster if you take these walks daily. Please do not overdo it, though," her mother instructed.

Mother and daughter talked about other issues before hanging up.

Thomas was holding a book titled "The Origins of Mankind"." He learnt that childbirth, also known as labour, parturition, and delivery, was the completion of pregnancy, where one or more fetuses exit the internal environment of the mother through what is usually called normal birth, through the vagina or via caesarean section, popularly known as C-section.

There were concerns that when the public healthcare facilities deteriorated in Zimbabwe many doctors performed the C-section, even when the patient was not in any danger, or when there was no evidence to suggest that there was need for it. The procedure was done for US$2 000. This became a lucrative business to the extent that many expecting mothers ended up crossing the Limpopo just to give birth.

"Hey babe, I wish you a normal delivery, and I am praying to God that you be granted that wish. You have been operated on twice, and it is my humble request that God grants us this request," Thomas remarked.

Thomas read in "The Origins of Mankind" that vaginal birth (normal birth) is the most common mode of birth worldwide. It involves four stages of labour: the shortening and opening of the cervix during the first stage; descent and birth of the baby during the second; the birth of the placenta during the third; and the recovery of the mother and infant during the fourth stage, which is referred to as the postpartum.

Thomas narrated these stages like a professional. He wanted to ensure that when the baby came, he would be prepared and would know what was exactly happening. Suddenly, there was a loud scream. Nomsa felt a wave of unbearable pain cutting through her. Immediately, Thomas knew that it was the first stage, characterised by abdominal partying or also backpain in the case of back labour that typically lasts half a minute and occurs every 10 to 30 minutes. Contractions gradually become stronger and closer together. Since the pain of childbirth correlates with contractions, the pain becomes more frequent and stronger as the labour progresses. The second stage ends when the infant is fully expelled. The third stage is the birth of the placenta. The fourth stage of labour involves the recovery of the mother, delayed clamping of the umbilical cord, and monitoring of the neonate.

Labour pains have both visceral and somatic components. During the first and second stages of labour, uterine contractions cause stretching and opening of the cervix. This in turn triggers visceral pain in the inner cervix and lower segment of the spine. Somatic pain is triggered at the end of the first and second stages by pain receptors that supply the nerves on the vaginal surface of the cervix, resulting from stretching, distention, and tearing of the vagina, perineum, and pelvic floor. Compared to visceral pain, somatic pain is more resistant to opioid pain medication. Nitrous oxide may be used in hospitals and birthing centres for this reason.

Another wave of pain ran through and it was clear to Thomas that they were gravitating towards the inevitable. He dialled for a taxi to take his wife to hospital. They went to Xuma Teaching Hospital in Johannesburg along Bree Street in the city centre. Thomas had registered his wife at the hospital for a safe delivery. A train of cars meandered through the city, providing a spectacular view of a country with first world infrastructure. However, poverty was in the same vein a characteristic of the great nation.

The driver entered through the main entrance speeding to the maternity ward. Thomas completed the paperwork while the nurses took Nomsa to the observation rooms. She was breathing heavily; the pain was unbearable. The baby was on the way, and she had mixed emotions. A part of her was excited that finally she was going to deliver her firstborn child, a boy for that matter. Her husband was increasingly getting worried about the continuity of his legacy as a man. He wanted a boy to continue with his legacy. He wanted his bloodline to be carried forward for generations to come.

"Hey babe, I am dome with the paperwork," Thomas said, his face glowing.

He had not attempted to conceal his joy that finally he was going to be a father. There were so many things that he wanted to do with his son.

Nomsa wanted to respond but the now frequent pain would not allow her. She lay there, quiet; a faded smile on her face. The nurse came to examine her to see if the baby was within the required centimetres.

"The baby is on its way. We got to move you ma'am," Sister Spumuzile warned.

At that moment, there was commotion. A group of South Africans entered the hospital.

"We come in peace. All that we want is for foreigners to leave this hospital. We don't care what your condition is; please leave in peace," one man, who appeared to be the leader, said calmly but authoritatively.

There was panic as doctors begged the angry Dudula gang to have mercy towards patients who were in critical condition, but all that was in vain.

"Look here, sir, we are doctors and our duty is to save life, why don't you allow us to stabilise the critical ones then we can discharge them," one doctor begged.

The members of the Dudula outfit went bed-by-bed and ward-by-ward asking for identification and ordering people to leave the hospital. When they got to Nomsa, they looked at her, shaking with fear and pain. She was afraid that they were going to expel her, which would have meant death. They left her alone and moved two metres away, then turned back. It was clear that they had had a change of heart.

"Ma'am, if you are a foreigner, please leave this place," the voice cut through her.

She wanted to move but she was in much pain. The baby was almost coming, but no one in the mob cared. She was forced to march out of the hospital. Thomas carried his wife; she screamed in agony—both physical and emotional.

Thomas walked to the gate, holding his wife. They wondered what to do next. He looked around to have a clearer view of the situation. A mob was gathering to see what was happening, and when he put her down, the waters broke. The baby was coming. Blood flowed profusely into a nearby drainage system. A cat licked the fresh blood, and loitered to see if there could be something else to eat.

"Babe, I am tired. I can't do this, hey; it's painful," Nomsa complained.

"Hold on babe you can do it, the Lord is with us. We are not alone," Thomas said, in a sharp urgent yet desperate voice.

He knew the odds against him, but he wanted to save his son and wife.

Nomsa was getting tired. The situation was getting desperate, yet people gathered to photos and videos and posting them on social media platforms like Facebook, X and Instagram, instead of assisting. Almost immediately, the internet was ablaze with likes and comments, some mean and others sympathetic. None of that mattered to Nomsa and Thomas.

Nomsa summoned all the strength she could muster, and, in spite of the excruciating pain, pushed once; then again. She felt him coming—their baby boy. Thomas became the midwife to her, assisting his wife to deliver, amid the hate and love in a foreign land. There was blood everywhere, but it didn't matter. Their boy was in the world now, against all the odds.

The video footage posted on the internet had prompted Zimbabwean doctors living in South Africa to react. They had set up a facility to cater for Zimbabweans in critical condition but failing to access medical care. As the Almighty God willed it, Nomsa and her baby, whom they named Thomas Junior, were, thus, safe.

A week later, the newly born Thomas Junior was cooing, unaware of the danger his mother faced to deliver him.

During the later stages of gestation, there is an abundance of oxytocin, a hormone known to evoke feelings of contentment, reductions in anxiety, and feelings of calmness. Oxytocin is further released during labour when the foetus stimulates the cervix and vagina, and it is believed that it plays a major role in the bonding of a mother to her infant as well as in the establishment of maternal behaviour.

The father of the child also has an increase in oxytocin levels following contact with the infant. Parents with higher oxytocin levels are more responsive and 'in synch' in their interactions with their infants. The act of nursing a child also causes a release of oxytocin to help the baby get milk easily from the nipple. Perhaps, that's why even after all the pain and suffering, Nomsa was excited to hold the child in her arms.

Chapter 9

The following morning Nomsa's issue was in the news, prompting debate on the handling of foreigners by the South African authorities.

"A brave Zimbabwean woman gave birth in the street outside Xuma Teaching Hospital in Johannesburg after being chased by the Dudula mob," reported the South African Cable News (SACC).

The SACC' panel discussion on the issue was chaired by Mpho Sigudu, a renowned presenter and human rights activist and sustainability author The speakers were Professor Desmond Zulu, an academic in African History, Doctor Nkululeko Mkhize , the Dean of the Faculty of Humanities and Social Sciences at Zwale University and Mr Mfundo Dhlamini, Head of International Migration in the Department of Immigration, and Sipho Mokoena, a socialite known for criticising the portrayal of fellow black Africans as criminals, job stealers and creators of havoc at public healthcare institutions in South Africa.

"Good morning, ladies and gentlemen. I want to thank you for joining us in this crucial discussion at such a short notice. And I must say, I have annoyed Dr Nkululeko Mkhize the most," Mpho remarked.

"Let me start with you Mr Dhlamini. What is your take on the video footage of a Zimbabwean woman seen giving birth in the street just outside the Xuma Teaching Hospital? Unfortunately, due the nature of the content, we cannot play it here, but I understand that all of you have had a chance to view it," Mpho opened the discussion, gesturing with his hands to emphasise the matter.

"Good morning viewers, at the Department of Immigration, we encourage all travellers to make sure they have requisite documentation. It is not clear whether Nomsa did or did not have proper documents for travel and living in South Africa.

"However, the matter at hand here is that of denial of service; a pregnant woman being pulled out of the maternity ward and thrown out of hospital; and the husband forced to deliver the baby," he said in shaky voice, fighting back tears.

There was silence for a moment then he continued, a bit composed now, "Prisoners are treated better than the manner we treated this woman. According to reports, she had registered to deliver there, and the husband was a holder of genuine papers, allowing him to stay in South Africa with his family."

Mpho was not ready. He wasn't prepared for what came in the opening remarks. He found himself fighting back tears but he had to be strong. He was the moderator, so he wasn't supposed to be emotional; he had to take charge.

"You make interesting observation right there, Mr Dhlamini. These people were treated unfairly. But others argue that foreigners, especially Zimbabweans, are invading our space and taking up jobs that should be given to South Africans as well as putting pressure on the healthcare infrastructure that is supposed to serve locals," Mpho followed it up.

Professor Desmond Zulu was itching to respond. As soon as Mpho was done he charged.

"Mpho, you made a very important observation there. The Zimbabwean government has a responsibility to rehabilitate and improve its economy, create jobs and absorb all its working class.

"The strain on public service is unbearable; the Zimbabwean government should do something about all this, rather than offloading all its citizens here," he said.

"That said, we must look at the context of the incident at hand. This incident has nothing to do with foreigners; its angry South Africans taking their frustrations on Zimbabweans. I do not think the solution is removing Zimbabweans from our economy. Many of them have been naturalised and are now a part of our community.

"For a person who left Zimbabwe 10 years ago, for example, if you deport him or her, they will still come back as they have moved on. South Africa is their new home," Prof Zulu added.

Dr Mkhize was taking notes.

"Before and after its independence in 1980, Zimbabwe was pivotal in the fight against apartheid. It was a critical Frontline State, with nationalist movements ZANU and ZAPU and their military wings ZANLA and ZIPRA, respectively, assisting South African cadres; using its territory for sanctuary, training, and launching attacks into South Africa. In their moments of desperation, South Africans needed their neighbours to rescue them," Dr Mkhize said.

"Dr Mkhize, many admit that the role played by Zimbabwe and, indeed, other African countries, is commendable and South Africans are grateful for that. However, the question is: Does the role played by Zimbabwe in the liberation struggle culminating in the independence of South Africa gives Zimbabweans an endless right to settle here illegally?" Mpho fired.

Before Dr Mkhize could respond, there was a commercial break. The discussion was now heated.

After two minutes, Dr Mkhize was back.

"Thank you for the question, Mpho. To understand the full extent of the role played by Zimbabwe at the time, we should understand that Zimbabwean liberation movements like ZAPU allied with the ANC of South Africa, with ZIPRA (ZAPU's military wing) and ANC's uMkhonto weSizwe (MK) sharing bases and logistical networks, particularly in areas like Gwayi and Matopo (Matobo)," he reflected.

"After independence in 1980, Zimbabwe became a formidable and crucial rear base for the ANC's **MK**. ZAPU's **ZIPRA**, offered safe houses, transport, and weapons caches. Zimbabwean individuals and groups provided simulated IDs, passports, and transport for **MK** cadres; helping them move weapons and personnel. Had it not been for Zimbabwe, South Africa would have taken longer to get freedom. Thus, we owe it to the people of Zimbabwe.

"And, just as we were battling the injustices of that time, so are Zimbabweans coming to seek refuge in our country-," as Dr Mkhize was elaborating, Mpho interrupted.

"Dr Mkhize, we all understand that. But what is the time limit for someone who has assisted in the past to keep holding on? Is it a lifetime ransom?

Sipho was dying to contribute, and as soon as Mpho gave the greenlight she took over.

"Good morning viewers! Thank you, Mpho for inviting me here. Operation Dudula says it is protecting the heart and soul of our motherland and that it is defending jobs as well as healthcare and security infrastructure from being overwhelmed by foreigners coming from failed states like Zimbabwe.

"This message is reasonable at face value. Understandably, the frustration is so real that everyone feels it. But what happens when frustration becomes a basis for crafting policy without scientific research to back it up? Sipho remarked.

"Are you saying the actions are not supported in any way, Sipho? Many people argue that they are fighting crime, mostly blamed on foreigners," Mpho said.

A grin cutting across her face, Sipho sat on the edge of her seat.

.

"Numbers don't lie, Mpho," she cut in. "South Africa has a population of circa sixty million, with both documented and undocumented migrants constituting between four and five percent of that. Surprisingly, such an insignificant constituency is said to have taken centre stage. Foreigners are being blamed for everything; from unemployment, to overloaded clinics and criminal activities. Would you consider that a true reflection or it's just convenient to do so?" She asked.

Sipho paused briefly to gauge the impact of her words. Convinced that everyone was keenly following, she continued.

"Most migrants in South Africa are not in 'highly paying employment' per se. In fact, more than eighty percent of them work in informal sectors such as domestic employment, street vending, construction and retail.

"These jobs are often unregulated and severely underpaying, raising concerns on how that creates labour gaps. In such a system, cheap and unprotected labour becomes profitable and attractive. An inclination towards foreign nationals willing to accept such jobs at the expense of locals becomes unavoidable.

"We may as well talk of wage growth and local skills development, but that should not be confused with migration issues which are rather labour enforcement-inclined. Another concern is safety. People ask why there is a sharp increase in informal settlements, unregistered businesses, and visitors overstaying on their visas, or continued illegal stay in South Africa," she said.

"What is the answer to that?" Mpho asked.

"Well, the answer is South Africa's dysfunctional legal system. There are over 95 000 people seeking asylum, with the backlog increasing, which may take up to four years to clear. Following the law looks reasonable, but the legal route is broken and non-functional.

"Another flashpoint is healthcare. There is a shared belief that migrants are overwhelming the healthcare system, especially clinics and hospitals. However, results from surveys by medical experts and non-governmental organisations are to the contrary. Undocumented migrants shy away from public clinics and hospitals, fearing arrest, possible deportation and ill-treatment. Hence, the argument that the South African healthcare system is being crippled by migrants is not only false but illogical.

In any case, the problem stems from exclusion, poor communication and underfunded systems," Sipho hit the nail in.

"Wow! That's mind-blowing. I hadn't looked at it from that angle. I suppose nobody had taken time to explore it from a more informed research-based approach," Mpho said, adding, "You have three minutes to wind up, and we will have reactions, then we open our phone-in lines."

"As I draw to a close, let me talk about western migrants, a topic many avoid. Migrants from Europe, North America, Australia, and some of the Baltic States, are here in our beloved motherland, living in well-resourced leafy suburbs, and enjoying favourable exchange rates. They also have access to world class private hospitals, yet public anger is only narrowing to low-income African migrants.

'So, the challenges faced by South Africa today are more to do with a malfunctioning labour market regulation system, which creates backlogs in immigration and partial application of the law," Sipho concluded to a round of applause from fellow panellists for a balanced well-articulated discussion.

"Wow! This is great debating—valid points raised there," Mpho commented. . "Our phone-in lines are now open. Let us hear what are viewers have to say."

"Good morning, Mpho! I was touched by this woman's story. But to be honest, Zimbabweans should just go back home. South Africa belongs to South Africans. I agree with Dr Mkhize that we got tremendous assistance from Zimbabwe during our struggle against apartheid, for which we are boundlessly grateful. However, my view is that it isn't right for South African to be ransomed and blackmailed for past events," said the first caller only identified as Sbu.

"Sbu, still on that; there are concerns that some migrants have inter-married and now have families here, while others have left their countries a long time ago. How can this be resolved? Mpho asked.

Sbu appeared to be listening carefully to Mpho at the other end of the line.

"The only solution is mass deportation of undocumented Zimbabweans," he answered without hesitation.

Jotting something on a pad on the polished hardwood desk, Mpho nodded.

"When you say Zimbabweans, do you push the notion that there are no Chinese, German, British, or French, among other nationals, who are illegal immigrants in South Africa?" Mpho asked, but Sbu had already signed out.

There was another caller; this time a woman named Sibongile Zulu.

"Zimbabwe is a rich nation with vast deposits of gold in all its ten provinces. It has platinum group resources; lithium, silver, palladium, copper, coal, and diamonds. It was once the breadbasket of Africa. Its tourism is vibrant. Above all, it is a peaceful, stable and tranquil nation," Sibongile reasoned.

"For a nation with such abundant resources, it is, therefore, baffling why it cannot extricate itself from the deep, entrenched poverty of its people."

"Zimbabweans have money but Zimbabwe has no money. There is a lot of corruption in that country. People drive latest cars at the expense of service delivery," another caller, HP, fumed.

During the interlude, Dr Mkhize said: "I wasn't yet done on how Zimbabwe helped South Africa achieve independence. Diplomatically and politically, Zimbabwe, under the late President Robert Mugabe, actively supported the ANC's efforts, using its new international legitimacy to advocate against apartheid, though its own internal politics later became complex.

"Zimbabwe's government helped internationalise the regional struggle, creating a strong solidarity network. The same way Zimbabwe asked our great nation to call for the unconditional removal of sanctions is the same manner in which we, as South Africans, reeling from the gruesome and burdensome weight of apartheid, asked Zimbabwe to help stop the needless loss of life in South Africa."

There was another caller coming in as Zap.

"Hey guys; you are being too soft with these foreigners. South Africa is for South Africans; all foreigners, whether they have papers or not, should just leave our country. We want our peace and jobs. Now, they are even taking our women and starting businesses in areas we should be benefitting from," Zap said.

The Facebook page was ablaze with comments. Some tagging hearts and likes whenever f driving out of foreigners was mentioned.

"We need them out like now," one KKG commented.

"The government has no clue regarding the issue of foreigners. There is nothing wrong with foreigners being here, but they should be documented and allowed to work in areas where we have shortages of manpower," one Simon opined.

Messages from the WhatsApp line were read randomly.

"The way the woman was treated showed me that we are a nation of savages. Chasing a pregnant woman from a maternity ward is the pits; even lions have respect for a delivering animal. Why are we so violent and lack character," Read a message from Naps.

A message from Gabriel read: "Dudula is a bunch of idiots; cowards who are afraid of the real people holding on to power and resources. If they are bold, they should take over companies and farms, and let's see if they will succeed in that."

The message ended with an angry emoji.

Message from Lunela: "I feel for the woman and her husband; forced to deliver their child in the open like a dog. No matter how much we are angry, attacking women and children shows that we are weak and evil."

Again, the message ended with an emoji of a man raising the middle finger.

Turning to the panel, Mpho asked: "Any final remarks under one minute?

Prof Zulu was the first to comment: "My view is that Dudula is an illegal organisation. Their act was barbaric and must be condemned in the strongest terms. This does not, however, mean that we are open for abuse by anybody.

"The solidarity of our brothers and sisters during our struggle for independence is appreciated; and for that we are eternally grateful. But we implore other African countries to progress and for leaders to build functional structures for their people. As South Africa, we will continue assisting, as we have always done, through investment companies in Zimbabwe, particularly in the retail, mining and agriculture value chains.

"South Africa has assisted Zimbabwe immensely through calling for the removal of the devastating economic sanctions imposed by the West on the behest of the United States and the European Union."

"Let's hear from Mr Dhlamini. Your final remarks, sir? Mpho said looking at his watch.

Mr Dhlamini. Cleared his throat, then said: "Well, like I have indicated in my earlier remarks, we encourage all travellers to use official documentation. Our responsibility is not to comment on how the government interacts with its citizens. However, looking and reflecting on the video, I believe that humanity should never act like that on one of its one. No one deserves such inhuman treatment, never.

"I beseech the government of South Africa to press charges against those goons. The world is watching while we treat fellow

Africans like that. The act give currency to the remarks by the US President, Donald Trump, that there is genocide in our country. How do you think this will be interpreted?

"We have given too much ammunition to the world, and when things backfire, we should not cry foul. Lastly, the push by the US to sanction our country may result in some of us needing to seek refuge in other countries."

Mr Dhlamini spoke passionately.

Dr Mkhize was the last to speak.

"In closing, I want to say Zimbabwe's involvement evolved from being a theatre of war to a vital sanctuary and support system for the ANC and its allies; demonstrating deep solidarity with the South African liberation struggle, a commitment sometimes overlooked in historical narratives.

"Let no man, woman, or child be deceived that we are enemies of each other. For, we have the Ngoni people settled permanently in Zambia. Are they to be humiliated for seeking sanctuary in Zambia, and for having no valid papers? No, they are recognised by the leadership of that country as citizens. We also have the Ndebele people, who migrated from South Africa, living in Zimbabwe having three whole provinces to themselves—Bulawayo, Matabeleland North, and Matabeleland South, as well as parts of the Midlands.

"They have papers now and are recognised as Zimbabweans, but when they crossed over, they did not have any. They were Africans roaming their motherland. We have the Nyathi people who migrated from Tanzania, some of whom are called Phiri, some of whom settled in Zambia, while others crossed into the Rusape area of Zimbabwe.

"The borders created for the convenience of colonialists shouldn't determine the way we relate to each other. Imagine a Tswana, Sotho, Shangani, Ndebele or Venda person living in Zimbabwe, requiring a passport to visit relatives in South Africa.

Honestly, this cannot be," Dr Mkhize deepened the conversation to its conclusion.

Chapter 10

Nancy and Sharon had a lot of catching up to do, with the latter having gathered information on visa applications. It was such a long checklist for the two friends.

"Ok girl, put me down," Nancy said.

Before Sharon could respond, Jeff called. Nancy rolled her eyes in annoyance. She told him that she would call back, but it was almost end of day before she did so. Jeff was getting worried, considering the issue of the mishandled luggage in the morning. Jeff had taken interest in Nancy but they had not managed to spend time together, so there were so many issues to be cleared out.

"Hello Jeff; how are you doing?" Nancy finally said in that soft voice only reserved for people she respected or loved.

"Nancy, are you ok my dear?' Jeff responded.

"I am well, Jeff. Thank you for everything. How was your day?"

"My day was fantastic. I am just worried about you, my dear. How is mum holding up?" Jeff asked with ease.

Nonetheless, the questions reminded Nancy of how untruthful she was. She had forgotten that she had rushed for a medical emergency. And, now here she was; needing to be charged up and create a narrative that goes with the lies she had been cooking all along.

There was silence, then the WhatsApp call was terminated after Nancy switched off data and put the phone on airplane mode. This was a trick that many people played if they did not want to speak to the person on the phone. That way, Nancy reconstructed her lies.

"Hello Jeff. I am sorry we have been interrupted by the network here. Mum is stable but still frail. We took her for medical attention and she is now under observation. We hope she will fully recover soon and be discharged," Nancy lied.

For some reason, she found herself shaking.

"Keep me posted, my dear." Jeff said encouragingly before terminating the call.

Nancy wondered if her lies were accepted or Jeff just decided to be quiet.

When she put the phone down, Sharon looked at her intently and burst into laughter.

"You know, you have matured like wine. We used to lie about little things, but I see you have graduated to a grandmaster. You lied about mum being ill, got an air ticket, and here you have Jeff on speed dial. He can easily send you money if you ask for it. You are a pro my dear," Sharon said, looking at her friend in a combination of admiration and envy.

The following three weeks saw the two running around; applying for sponsorships sponsorship, sitting the International English Language Testing System (IELTS) exams, going for medical examinations, signing contracts and submitting passports for visas processing. Their visa applications were approved after seven working days.

Chapter 11

Nancy dashed to Victoria Falls on Jeff's invitation. He had changed his departure date so as to spend some time with Nancy. The two spent two nights together. Realising that Jeff only wanted sex, she turned him down and flew back to Harare.

Nancy wove through the crowd at the arrivals gate after the mishandled baggage experience. A large group of adults in orange T-shirts packed the terminal. Songs erupted as dancers in different shades of orange and green swept onto the floor, gyrating to the beat. Placards flung into the air, as fans cheered and shouted. Posters, fans chanting and security lining the corridors left no doubt that a high-profile person had arrived. Journalists huddled together, flashing cameras and holding out microphones. Selfie-pods and phones went up as everyone tried to catch the perfect shot of the superstar. A rumble ran through the crowd as murmurs and whispers spread.

Nancy caught sight of a figure striding through the throng, flanked by beefy bodyguards. A man with glossy dark skin, a pointed chin and bunny teeth waved at the onlookers. His orange flared pants and half-buttoned leopard-print shirt exposed tufts of chest hair.

Nancy shuddered at the tufts of curly hair peeking from his shirt. They reminded her of her ex — that jerk with his hair fetish. The thought made her skin prickle. She looked down, forcing the image from her mind. Then she met another surprise: small green sneakers, ridiculous for a man that tall. Staring at his absurd shoes, she giggled. Then her stomach flipped. That face. She had seen it countless times popping up on YouTube, Facebook, and all her other social feeds.

Afro Kassa, the Ethiopian Afrobeats sensation, had touched down for his maiden tour of Zimbabwe. Journalists clustered with cameras, scrambling to keep ahead of the horde of fans snapping selfies. Afro Kassa's previous show had been cancelled following a ban because of his radical remarks on sexuality. Everyone deserves a second chance. Everyone except her ex, of course. Even Nancy and Sharon were reviving their friendship.

The cheers and chants were enough proof that the fans adored Afro Kassa. Fans from across generations swarmed the place. Nancy pushed her suitcase with one hand and adjusted her backpack with the other, manoeuvring through the crowd. She had tucked her phone into her bra, keeping an eye out for anyone brushing too close. Her fingers tightened with every accidental bump. She knew pickpockets loved events like this,snatching phones like in the chaos.. Still, she felt safe, confident that her luggage was secure. She tried to push through the crowd, but the throng slowed every step. One man walked alongside her, matching her pace. Finally reaching the door, she sighed. But the man was still there. She had a feeling that someone was watching her but she ignored it.

Suddenly, someone yelled, "Bluetooth! Bluetooth! Orange leggings!"

Startled, Nancy froze and tuned sideways, scanning for anyone else wearing orange leggings like hers. She then stared at herself and clutched her bag tighter. Another tactic of pickpockets. They create commotion. She took one more step.

The man shouted again, "Bluetooth, sister!"

The throng of fans joined in the search of the 'Bluetooth' device. The man who had been yelling came up to Nancy and whispered. She became self-aware and looked between her thighs, then brushed her bum with one hand. In coordination with the yelling, a bulky man caught up with the man who had been following Nancy. The culprit wore an orange T-shirt that read, "Big Boy Limited." In an instant, everyone forgot about Afro Kassa. Phones flashed and people recorded videos. A crowd gathered around the scene, whistling and hurling insults at the man. They shouted at him, mocking his T-shirt: "Keep your big boy inside your pants!" "Limit your big boy!"

The man was accused of having a sexual encounter with Nancy via an invisible connection called 'Bluetooth' pairing, or *mubobobo* in Shona. This practice is common in public places, where it is hard to tell the perpetrator or even realise that one would have been Bluetoothed. This is common on packed buses as well. In some instances men and women line up in the aisle, face-to-bum. In others, the spaces are so cramped that people stand back-to-back, each pressed toward the window. This practice is powered by juju, with men usually being the culprits. The legal system grapples with cases of mubobobo, due to a total lack of evidence. Often, the act is written off as witchcraft, which is complex issue in Zimbabwean statutes. In courts of law, it's impossible to address. The act is considered a non-consensual, non-physical sexual assault. Some traditional courts handle it, though. Legal redress, however, is inconsistent. Most people dismiss it as queueing fatigue.

Nancy remembered all the stories she had heard about mubobobo. She looked down to avoid the phone cameras. The crowd's attention shifted to the culprit, as people pulled out their phones to record him. A police officer near Afro Kassa shrugged and dismissed him. Again, there was no evidence. Murmurs of disappointment spread through the fans as they refocused on the celebrity.

In that commotion, Nancy slipped out of the throng. She walked up to the small black car Sharon had arranged for her. It sat in the parking lot, exactly as Sharon had described.

Puzzled, Nancy wondered why a Honda Fit would have a personalised number plate. When the driver stepped out, it all became clearer. Even his belt and cap had the same name. They shook hands, and she slid into the back seat. Sharon was already there, and another lady sat up front. In a quick round of introductions, Nancy met the other woman, Rudo, sister of one Detective Mike.

The driver, T1 worked as a fitness trainer. Most of his clients were women, especially from overseas. He trained them to keep fit while visiting the motherland. He also offered extended services, including massage and happy endings. He claimed he kept women fit through and through, hence the Honda Fit. Sharon had used his services for a while, and this was one of the extras he would do for loyal clients. Taken aback by the information overload, Nancy reconnected with her friend, clapping, holding hands, and taking selfies. She told them about her ordeal with the 'Bluetooth' man. Rudo suggested her brother, the detective, could help. Nancy leaned forward as Rudo dialled her brother.

The detective empathised with Nancy but explained that there was never enough evidence to catch any alleged perpetrator. The two ladies squeezed her hand and offered reassurance. After an awkward silence, they all burst into laughter.

"Welcome to Harare," they said. The car drove to Sharon's place, and that night, the women unpacked their stories till dawn.

Their tickets to Heathrow were all paid up. All three of them. Sharon teased that it was odd Jeff hadn't called Nancy after she landed.

Nancy fetched her phone from the dresser and called. When his wife answered, she erupted into a string of curses. Sharon, who sat next to her on the bed, restrained her with a sudden kiss. Taken aback, Nancy froze for a moment, then kissed her back. Regaining her senses, she pushed Sharon away and slapped her.

Nancy's anger drained from her in an instant, leaving her dizzy. Her fingers trembled; her phone slipped from her hand and landed on the bed. Rudo missed the whole incident as she was in the bathroom.

"What was that about?" she asked on her return.

"Yuck!" Jeff is married. Can you believe it?"

"I'm sorry. I couldn't think of any other way to stop you. Never fight another woman over a man," Rudo said. "Well, we are leaving in two days' time. You'll find a good man out there."

That night, Nancy tossed and turned, thinking about the warmth of that kiss and how it made her feel. It could be good that she was going to start over again in the diaspora. Firstly, the mubobobo man, then this unusual kiss. Surely, the universe was telling her to leave. She smiled that she didn't go viral on social media after the airport incident.

Chapter 12

Excitement turned to anxiety the moment Nancy and her friends touched down at Heathrow Airport.

Her stomach knotted as she scanned the crowded arrivals hall, half-expecting another incident. She walked so close to her friends that she nearly stumbled over her own feet. The walk to the exit felt like a marathon, her pulse hammering in her ears. When they spotted the man picking them up, her shoulders relaxed, and she let out a soft whimper. Her friends glanced at her, brows knitting.

She gave a shaky smile and a nod. She struggled to keep a straight face. They all chuckled. Her friends reminded her that she had left the unruly men of Harare behind. She had landed abroad where the airport radiated glitz.

The ride to their shared accommodation was quiet, broken only by soft yawns and the drag of jet lag. For the first time since landing, Nancy let herself relax, leaning back against the seat and closing her eyes as streaks of sunlight sifted through the window. They headed to Manchester. Their driver laughed, saying there was more to the place than football, though he hadn't been to a Manchester Derby. The city was a patchwork of neighbourhoods, each with its own charm; and it would take a lifetime to explore them all.

Chapter 13

Farai, Gabriel and Takudzwa debated whether to settle in the Mbombela District or further up the province of Mpumalanga. Mbombela, the capital of the province, was popular for producing citrus fruits, while the highveld took pride in summer cereals and legumes. Soya beans topped the list. Combined, the lowveld and highveld regions of Mpumalanga solidified its agricultural footprint in South Africa.

With all three boys raised in Nyanga where fruits and crops abound, they were indifferent on where to go. Growing up, they herded all other livestock except sheep. The trio's final decision relied on comfort rather than suitability. After crossing the treacherous Limpopo River, they had faced their largest hurdle ever. They had confronted and overcame their worst fear. They reflected on how their friend Simon had chosen fear over fighting for a better future. The pain of relying on one's parents for data bundles, let alone credit to make a call, was as real as it was frustrating. They wanted a better life. Anything else didn't matter. Dreams of brighter days abounded.

Mpumalanga, one of South Africa's most productive agricultural regions, offered plenty of seasonal work. An earthy scent of cow dung welcomed them in Amersfoort, a busy farming hub surrounded by vast fields of soya beans and other crops. In three days, they'd found jobs and settled into farm life.

With only one week in Amersfoort, their phones flooded with requests for money. A legion of sob stories followed. Still, the thrill of earning and standing on their own feet outweighed the pressure. Each icy morning, the boys rose before dawn. Soya bean fields became their favourite place. By sunrise, they would have joined the rest of the farm workers. Frost on the ground, breath white in the dark, they would march on.

* * *

Someone coughed. Another muttered, "Yho, it's cold." Pots clanged softly in the shacks, pap reheating and water boiling. Enough water for tea. A bath only made sense at night after a long day of toil. Bachelors were often too exhausted to shower and too carefree to bother. Only the married put effort in bathing after work because their wives insisted. On weekends, everyone bathed as they were off work and mingled. The shacks buzzed with chatter, laughter, and the occasional drunken brawls. Sleepovers and hook ups happened too, quick and quiet. A breather before Monday dragged them back to the fields--all work and no play.

Monday always came too soon. The trio had rummaged old boots from the communal shed. Uniforms were new though. Gabriel pulled on his torn boots; the soles patched with tape. He sipped his rich creamy tea, still half-asleep, watching steam curl through the cracks of the tin walls. He savoured each sip having last drank tea in Zimbabwe. Farai and Takudzwa preferred black coffee, like their women.

A rooster crowed near the fence of their shack. As if on cue, they wiped their mouths with the backs of their hands, grabbed their hats, and stepped into the morning breeze. By first light, the fields were alive, men and women bending low between the rows. Dew soaked their sleeves. Clumps of black earth clung to their hands, wet from last night's irrigation. The older women led the rhythm, with everyone else in sync. It lightened the load as their hands moved through rows of soya beans, spinach and cabbage. A tractor roared nearby, spitting smoke.

The foreman's whistle shot through the air. "Faster! You, lazy assholes!" he shouted. Gabriel gritted his teeth and punched the ground. Farai stared at him with the corner of his eye. Of the three friends, Gabriel carried his temper on steroids. His mother often warned him that anger would be his downfall. He'd better stay clear of booze and women. He dismissed her as speaking gibberish. His life, his rules. But here he stood; hunched like wheelbarrow and tossed about by a fellow countryman in a foreign land.

A young man of exceptional intelligence, he scored 14 points at Advanced-Level. He could have become a biochemical engineering student at the country's finest university, University of Zimbabwe, if only he had found the funding. Sadly, his distinctions didn't distinguish him on the farm. Now, he took orders in the fields.

You could work without thinking, without cracking your head. All you did was copy whatever the next person was doing. A job so menial that the only qualification required were two hands. The foreman barked orders non-stop depending on his mood.

At midday, they all rested under a dry acacia tree. Gabriel wiped sweat from his forehead. He shared his pap with Nozipho, who'd forgotten hers again. She came from Bulawayo, Zimbabwe's second largest city. They talked about home, the rains that never came, and her brother in Joburg, who promised to send money so she could join him.

The chitchat faded when the bell rang. Back to the fields. The sun sat directly overhead, scorching their clothes. By now, they were used to being sticky with sweat in the intense heat. Farm work does one of two things: it either makes you age faster, or it makes you feel younger.

Being the last day of the month, the boss's bakkie roosted by the fence. He watched from the driver's seat, elbow resting on the window. He talked on the phone, his cigarette glowing and fading between puffs. He watched like a scavenger, eyes darting across the field. When someone slowed, the horn blared. Everyone kept their heads bowed.

They kept moving, bending, sulking and frowning under their hats. By now, most had developed callouses. Babies cried from the shed. Only nursing mothers and smokers were allowed up to five short breaks. Morale had dipped. A husky voice sang a hymn. All the labourers joined in unison.

Even during wars, songs strengthen armed forces. One more push before calling it a day. The sun painted the field in warm bronze. Sacks lined up, scales clanking open on the tailgate where the boss now sat. The boss dropped his cigarette, grinding it under his boot before stepping down. He scanned the rows, counting. An eerie silence settled over the field, punctuated by heavy breaths.

The sun gleamed off the scales and the tops of the sacks as he declared, "Too light," on more than half of them. This gave him reason to underpay. A cliché trick.

Hearts pounded as the workers waited for their wages. Sweat glowed on their foreheads. The wage of sin is death, but the wage for toiling in this field was uncertainty. Some got half pay, some nothing. A few, the fastest, the favourites, earned a pat on the shoulder and a nod.

Gabriel, Farai and Takudzwa smiled when they received their envelopes. Finally, they could send money home, buy groceries, maybe even feel like men in charge of their lives. Enough of being men written on toilet signs.

Gabriel's jaw tightened as the boss lingered near Nozipho, too close for comfort. He groped her bum. She had begged her brother to bring her to Joburg, but he was busy wasting his money on Xhosa women. It was his money after all. Now, she silently endured. Gabriel's eyes blazed, fists clenching as he glared at the boss. He turned to his friends, trying to distract himself. Together they trudged to their shacks.

The rest walked home slowly, shoes slapping the dust, children were quiet now. Smoke rose from the hills; smell of wood fire and mealie meal waiting. They didn't talk much. Just the sound of shuffling feet, the soft cry of a baby, and the whistling of wind through the grass.

Gabriel sat outside their door, boots off, legs stretched. He watched the twilight fade to black. The sky always looked better in Nyanga, home. He had never lived in a shack until he arrived in South Africa.

His two friends joined him, smoking weed, talking about his crush on Nozipho, and reminiscing about home and the weekend's English Premier League results. Arsenal had beaten Liverpool again, leaving them stunned. The usual football banter followed: arguments over who deserved the trophy.

But even as they laughed, Gabriel's jaw remained tight. The image of his boss fondling Nozipho made his stomach churn. A knot coiled in his chest. He tried to push it down, to focus on the stories and jokes. Another day gone. Tomorrow would be the same, hard, hot, and endless. But he would still rise. They would all rise. For themselves, and for their parents back home. Their whole clans.

On the farms in Mpumalanga, work was all there was. And there was the distant hope that maybe, someday, it would be enough. And before dawn, they would rise again.

Chapter 14

Six months since arriving in Mpumalanga, Gabriel, Farai and Takudzwa's faces had grown fuller, and their bellies rounded. Callouses thickened on their hands. Their backs ached from the endless work, but they moved with more strength. The mornings were no longer icy. The sun climbed higher, baking rows of cabbages in warmth.

In those long, green lines, they encouraged each other and joked around. Even the foreman joked when he was high on dagga. The three friends preferred the tipsy foreman to the stern one. He liked to tease the workers, warning them not to behave like the snails nibbling on the cabbage leaves. Snails of all sizes clung to the leaves, chewing neat holes and inching along, always evading the hoes.

The locals laughed at the trio's reactions and dared them to try the snails, calling them "farm-fresh protein." Once cooked, they weren't slimy, a few of the men reassured them, glancing at their frowning faces. Crunchy and a little chewy, the snails tasted strange at first, surprisingly delicious. They laughed at the taste, daring each other to try some more.

Between bites and laughter, they had also blended to the rhythm of the farm: bend, pull, lift, repeat. Around them, fields of young soya beans, maize, and spinach crops swayed in the warm September sun. A patchwork of green stretching toward the horizon.

WhatsApp messages kept flooding in; one after another: school fees, food, clothes, even capital to start a business. Every month, another request for capital. Was the business just... the business of starting a business? One wondered.

At this ridiculous rate, next could be money for the dog's food and to fix potholes. Each notification felt draining. Farai particularly dreaded opening his messages. Uncles he had never met hunted him on WhatsApp and through friend requests on Facebook.

The three friends shared the same sentiments. They were under twenty-five and deserved a chance to shape their own destinies. To make mistakes. To find their own successes. And to act responsibly in whatever they pursued. Yet, every message from home tugged at the little they had, each one about demands, needs, and expectations that never let them rest.

Back home, it was common for people to laugh when you returned with nothing but a backpack, heading back to your parents' house. Decades in the diaspora, and all you had to show were a handful of fake labels and a single pair of original sneakers.

On the farm, life was insignificant, but the struggle was real. They huddled over their pittance of wages, counting coins and notes. They debated whether to buy fast food or send money home. A bucket of KFC felt like a victory, and a beer like a small rebellion. For a moment, they tasted freedom, until the next message notification.

By the time the September sun climbed higher, the farm was still. Something in the air tasted sour. Garbriel felt it in his gut. That Monday, the foreman barked as usual, but his voice was cracky. A group of older men whispered near the tractor, their voices tense. They spoke in isiZulu but Garbriel caught the word "strike". They were tired. Tired of being underpaid, of sweat stolen by the boss. Sick of empty promises. Sick of abuses. Sick of being used.

Danger thrilled Garbriel. Every instinct urged him to join, and he saw the same tension in his friends. Fear gripped their chests even as excitement pulsed through them. No papers. No rights. Always choose your battles. Garbriel wanted to punch the foreman and the boss, but he knew he had to keep his job, for now. His hands ached, his back burned, and the thought of another week scraping by on half wages tightened his chest. If all three friends stopped working, they could be sent away, or worse, handed over to Home Affairs and deported.

By noon, half of the workers had stopped moving. They leaned on hoes and shovels, chanting slogans, demanding the pay for last month. The foreman stormed out, his shirt half-tucked, half-hanging, fists pounding the metal table.

"You think I care about your little strike? Get back to work or get out!"

His voice cracked with anger, but it held no real power. The farm relied on them, illegal or not, and he knew it. He forgot he was also an immigrant. A son of the soil exploiting his own people on foreign land The locals could find jobs any day, though.

Gabriel stayed frozen for a moment, heart hammering. He looked at Nozipho and the others. They all set with chests out and heads held high. They continued to sing and dance. They even ate pap during work hours. Gabriel swallowed hard, dropped his hoe, and joined the demonstrations.

The foreman cursed, threatening to call the police, but Gabriel knew that the locals could attack them for not siding with them. They could kill you as a sell-out. If the farm called the authorities, he could be deported, lose the little he had gathered in this small, dusty village.

Still, the anger in him screamed louder than fear. He raised his voice in unison with the others.

"Enough! Enough! Enough!" they chanted.

The words felt heavy on Gabriel's tongue, yet liberating. The strike would be short. Dangerous. Maybe meaningless. But for the first time in months, he felt a refreshing surge of energy. He was born for this. The farm could threaten him, chase him away, and cheat him again. But today, he chose to stand, for himself and for Nozipho. He loved her.

By late afternoon, the foreman's fury had died down. He was ready to negotiate on his own terms. He called the leader of the workers and the others to the shed.

"If you think you can play games, think again," he hissed, pacing back and forth.

"No pay. No work. And you —" he pointed fingers at several men, including Gabriel, Takudzwa and Farai, "you don't belong here. You have papers? No. You have a family? Maybe. Doesn't matter. You walk, or I call the police."

Gabriel felt the blood drain from his face. His stomach knotted. Walking away meant losing the little he had. It meant losing the few rands he'd managed to save. And it meant putting himself at the mercy of the authorities. Staying meant hunger, back pain, and humiliation. In his dilemma, he glanced at Nozipho. Her eyes were blank, but her lips were pursed. In fact, everyone knew it wasn't really a choice.

* * *

Midmorning on Friday, wailing filled the farm. Everyone dropped what they were doing and ran toward the shed, where a man stood, speaking to the boss and other workers. He looked weary, out of place; an elderly man in a faded white coat. A hospital orderly.

The boss's face looked sullen. He removed his hat as the orderly spoke. Gabriel and other labourers quickly caught up with the news. All the men followed suit, removing their hats in silent remembrance.

A moment of silence. The boss asked, his voice sincere for the first time ever, "You came from the hospital?"

The man nodded. "Yes. I thought you should know what happened."

He shifted on his feet, eyes lowered.

"Bystanders later traced her to this farm. Nozipho had come to Emagweni Hospital early this morning... said her stomach hurt, had been hurting for a week."

The wailing continued, rising and falling like the wind over the fields. The small crowd continued to listen. Some froze, gasping; others shook their heads. The men clutched their tools, some covering their mouths.

"She reached the gate," he went on, coughing, "but that gang you hear on the news stopped her. What's wrong with our men and women? They chased her away, saying she must be treated in her own country."

One of the women in the crowd muttered, "She begged them, didn't she?"

The orderly gave a slow nod: "A few nurses tried to help, offering to admit her. But that lunatic threatened them. They couldn't do anything."

He rubbed his hands together as if to warm them.

"She collapsed right there on the road. A ruptured appendix. So sad. She was only nineteen. We couldn't revive her."

The foreman also sobbed. Gabriel listened in sombre silence, his head bowed.

"We found her phone," the orderly went on, softer now. "Called her brother. He talked to the police. He said he'll come here to collect her wages and belongings."

The wailing had grown fainter now, replaced by the dull hum of the wind through the fields.

The orderly looked around the shed, at the bowed heads, the quiet disbelief.

"That is the price of being a foreigner," he said.

Dust drifted in the light slanting through the acacia trees. After a moment, he added, almost to himself, "Ethics says no one should be denied medical attention, no matter their name or status. That's the Hippocratic Oath."

The boss hid his face in his hat. He called the man and the foreman inside, and the workers slowly dispersed.

* * *

That night, Gabriel sat with his friends outside their shack, boots off, staring at the dark hills. Farai's phone crackled with nostalgic Zimbabwean songs, children laughed in the distant, and women huddled, gossiping.

Gabriel felt defeated. His Nozipho. He could have done more to protect her. He should have given her money to go to his brother. He could never forgive himself.

The wind was cold, biting at his bare arms. He felt motivated to leave. Heading north, south, anywhere he could disappear and find work without a ruthless foreman breathing over him; a new place without constant reminders of Nozipho. Just anywhere he could earn without begging or fear. He had crossed the dangerous Limpopo River. Now, he knew he could face anything.

His hands itched to dig in the dirt, to earn. The farm had cheated him, yes, but it had also fed him. It had kept a roof over his head, even though it was tin and dust. He cursed himself for thinking about leaving, for letting fear and hope mix. But the thought of never seeing Nozipho at the farm hurt him.

By dawn, Gabriel had made a decision. He would leave. Alone this time. But not out of cowardice. He would leave because staying meant being trapped, like trophy fish. He would walk through the cold morning, past the shacks and along the gravel road, seeking better, greener pastures. He didn't know where he would go. He didn't know if he would find any pastures at all. But he knew one thing: staying on that farm, under the foreman's whistle, would mean losing himself, one day at a time. Staying meant that one day, either he or the foreman would go down. Forever.

He was ready to fight but not to be arrested for winning that fight. He always fought like a wounded bull. A heartbroken man is a dangerous man. He had to run away from himself.

Chapter 15

Before sunrise, Gabriel slipped out of the shack, walking on tiptoe and careful not to wake anyone. His backpack carried his few clothes, some leftover pap, and his money. He left a little note under Farai's phone.

The gravel crunched softly under his boots, and every sound felt loud in the cold morning. He paused at the edge of the road, listening. No foreman. No tractors. Only the wind and distant roosters.

He walked quickly, keeping close to the shadows of the shacks. The farm stretched behind him, fences and fields. He didn't look back. Each step felt like leaving a part of himself behind, his friends, Nozipho, the dust, the sweat, and the stolen wages. But also, it felt like claiming something he had yearned for all his life: true freedom.

Hours passed, the road twisting through hills and bushes. Gabriel's feet ached, his legs stiff, but he kept moving. Occasionally, he passed other workers, heading to the fields. Some recognised him and nodded. Others pretended not to notice him, for fear of his hot temper. He could have been going anywhere. It was common to have a day or two off-duty.

This time he chose to trust no one but himself. He could always phone his friends. Like how they all kept contact with Simon, their friend who had chickened out at the last minute of crossing to South Africa.

At midday Gabriel spotted a small village. He ducked into a café, the smell of garlic almost choking him. The owner gave him a quick glance, then turned back to the cash register, saying nothing. He bought an energy drink with coins he counted twice, eyes always on the door. He sipped his drink like it was an elixir. Gabriel closed his eyes, savouring the moment of freedom. The streets clamoured with people, some playing pool, others chatting at corners, and children running and laughing. Exactly what he needed. Here, no one could claim him, at least not yet. He expected his friends to call if they had airtime. Not everyone had phone credit to spare. Or if they cared.

Back at the farm, Farai and Takudzwa chuckled, guessing Gabriel had gone for a one-night stand with one of the girls, another way to get over losing Nozipho. He used to brag about their steamy episodes in her shack, the barns, even behind the boss's shed. Her death had shaken him so much that most nights he disappeared, gratifying his frustrations with whoever he could pay. A measly R50 usually sealed the deal.

That morning, the two friends assumed he'd gone out, like the past few nights, on one of his screwing sprees.

It was only after lunchbreak that Farai saw the note tucked under his phone. He hardly checked it in the mornings anymore. All those WhatsApp messages asking for money ruined his day. A legion of requests for money. The blackmail voice notes nauseated him, sulking each time he received one. Sometimes he shoved the phone under his pillow. Each message suffocated him. Always problems from home. Never mind his own. He was too busy breaking his back for people who didn't care if he was even well. Leaving Zimbabwe now felt like a death sentence in itself. Some days he wondered if it was worth all the toil. He could as well die a pauper.

Reading that goodbye note made Farai and Takudzwa realise the magnitude of their decision to cross the border. The note read:

Boys you have my number. I've had enough of this bullshit from these assholes. We didn't risk our lives across the Limpopo for this bullshit. I'm out. One love.

The two sank onto the bed. Gabriel's handwriting looking beautiful and almost legible for the first time. They had fought countless street fights growing up. Studied side by side through high school; braved the dangerous waters of the Limpopo, and survived police raids in Mpumalanga. They were also beaten by the cold and rain on the farm. Now, South Africa had separated them, as they had been separated from their families.

Time and circumstances test true friendship. We all go through our litmus tests. The inevitable. Fate.

"Let's call him... Call him. I only have call-me-backs. Good?" Takudzwa said, patting Farai's shoulder.

Chapter 16

Gabriel jumped onto the next bus to the nearest major town, Ermelo. It promised better opportunities, more work, more hustle, and new possibilities. During the hour-long ride, he scrolled through Facebook Marketplace, searching for affordable accommodation.

By evening, he slipped into the narrow space between two blocks of shops, the street noise muffled behind him. Cracked walls rose on either side, faded paint peeling, and a few tufts of grass pushed through the concrete. He ate the last of his pap, eyes tracing the long shadows stretching across the alley. The faint smell of grilled meat and smoke drifted from the nearby market. He struggled to ignore the tempting aroma. He had to save every cent, until he found another job.

Further up, three girls loitered, wearing only enough to cover the bare necessities. Their low chatter blended with the hum of the town. Behind him, the noise of the market faded. Silence. For the first time in months, he could breathe freely. Without asking permission. No foreman barking orders. No boss growling in his ear. No sudden visions of Nozipho haunting his eyes. He was alone, for now, in Ermelo.

Tomorrow he would walk further. He would look for work, even if it meant washing people's cars. Today, he had taken the first step. That phone call from his friends confirmed he had made the best decision for himself. His friends were content with the laid-back life on the farm, despite their misgivings about the ongoing exploitation. They were afraid. Fear of the unknown is a man's worst enemy. It destroys dreams. Gabriel would not let group mentality define his destiny. They had crossed the Limpopo River together, but in South Africa, each to his own. Still, he would have crossed alone if everyone else had turned back.

He patted himself on the back. He'd finally stepped away from mediocrity. And for the first time in a long time, he felt in charge of his life. A new life in Ermelo; a town where he was ready to do anything and everything to succeed, without the sweat. Yet, somewhere deep inside, Gabriel knew that leaving the farm didn't solve everything. But staying there would have solved nothing at all.

* * *

In Joburg, Adam, Nozipho's brother set off with Loliwe to arrange the collection of his sister's body. It was the longest drive of his life. No one can ever change the hands of time. He wished he could. He pinched himself for failing his sister, leaving her to die at the hands of merciless people. Women and men alike chased her like a dog. Back in the day, women were the epitome of kindness. They were sympathetic, especially of fellow women. Now, they exemplified hatred on steroids. Worse than men. End times. Such abominations.

When the undertaker opened the catalogue, Adam stared at it as if reading a blank page. Loliwe squeezed his hand. She had never seen him so down. She asked the undertaker questions as they went past the low-priced coffins. Swallowing hard, she pointed at a casket she wished someone had chosen for her parents. She stopped at the one made of polished mahogany, running her thumb across the edge.

"This one suits her," she murmured. Adam blinked, shaking on reflex. "It's... it's beautiful. Like her beautiful life cut short;

snatched by cruel people. What happened to Ubuntu? The price us orphans have to pay. An orphan in a foreign country. What a nightmare," he bemoaned.

They moved to the hearse selection. Again, Loliwe went ahead, walking to the finest, sleek cars. The kind of send-off her own parents never received. Parents stolen from her by that angry crowd in Soweto. Their crime? Being foreigners trying to make an honest living.

Adam bit his lips rubbing his hands, "Loliwe, you don't have to do all this."

She gave a little shrug: "Someone should. This is for Nozipho; my parents too."

Loliwe's hand hovered over the mahogany casket, and for a moment, she was that trembling child again. That fateful week, Loliwe was too young to give her own parents a decent burial. The memory hit her chest like fire, tightening her stomach and clenching her fists. She pushed the fury inside, hiding it from the world. She would never forgive the people who wronged her and her siblings.

Even now, Loliwe provided sexual gratification to men and women for a living, but the smell of any local client made her flinch. Every casket around her sliced her like a knife, reminding her of that tragic night and the child who had waited in vain for justice; justice for her parents and for all the other foreigners burnt alive. But now, power had changed hands. This was her game, and she had to play it well. In chess, a pawn could become a queen, and with the right timing, even topple a king. Rules of survival.

Loliwe met Adam on his second visit to the hotel where she did sex work. By then, she'd shifted her trade from risky house calls to hotel rooms. She reasoned that hotel bookings guaranteed her safety: CCTV, and a front desk clerk who'd remember her face if she disappeared. She'd watched *Vanished Without a Trace* too many times to ignore the risks of her business. Her industry thrived on competition and rivalry. She had to watch her back at all times.

Expanding the business to women had been her most profitable move. Her cash cow. She received high-profile clients through referrals. She never took anyone to her house. Again, for security. Usually, safety came in numbers. When she met Adam, he had grown weary of spending money on low-life girls.

He had planned to save — to bring his sister, Nozipho to live with him. Nozipho had nagged him to bring her to the city. He was working towards that when he moved from a rickety aluminium shack. He wanted her to stay at the farm, safer than the crooked streets of the City of Gold: the cramped houses, the tacky shebeens. He only wanted the best for her. He was a little too late. He had reassured her that a shack at the farm was better than a shack in the city.

On the evening that Adam hooked up with Loliwe, his boss had referred him to her. He was ready to spend every cent on this wonder woman. Rumour held that she also brought along toys and props just in case the client wanted to pay for extra services.

Walking up to that hotel room to meet Adam, Loliwe had a lingering sadness she couldn't place. She sat in the leather chair by the window and readied herself. Waited. The moment Adam walked in, her heart skipped. She rubbed her eyes fast and blinked like a Barbie Doll. To her, Adam looked like a mirror image of her father. His duplicate. Her father reincarnate. The resemblance was so uncanny that the pang of sadness she'd felt earlier returned. She froze. Then she downed a shot of whisky.

Loliwe always vetted her clients. She never took anonymous ones. Same reason she never saw more than two at a time. Without her father, she felt she had to protect herself at all costs, her gun always within reach. Yet, with Adam, she felt safe after ten minutes of staring at each other. With him, she felt a fatal attraction that went beyond a business transaction. One thing led to another. Now, she was a part of his life, organising his sister's funeral while lying about stopping her business. Her life, her rules. That's where her control lay. She still harboured a grudge against the people who killed her parents. Her business formed an important part of her revenge.

Chapter 17

Gabriel trudged through the crowded streets of Ermelo. The early sun burned at the back of his neck. His petite frame made it easier to blend in with the crowd. The few rands he had left pushed him from door to door, searching for work. He freshened up whenever he could, at public taps, careful to look presentable. He had always taken pride in being a smart boy, the reason girls had flocked to him back in high school. That confidence had thinned, worn away by guilt for leaving the farm. Still, he soldiered on, daring himself never to return.

He slept wherever he could: under the tin roofs of abandoned shacks, behind the supermarkets; anywhere he could stay out of sight. With no affordable shacks available, Gabriel had to make do with whatever shelter he could find. At times, in the early evenings, he stood on a dusty street corner, staring toward the distant hills of Amersfoort. Staring into oblivion.

Around him, children laughed and shouted, kicking tattered soccer balls between the shacks. Music thumped from nearby shebeens. Smoke from braais and cooking fires curled into the sky, carrying the aroma of chakalaka boerewors. Vendors whistled and hustled their goods along the street, shouting over the noise. Even the stray dogs pottered, sniffing for scraps. He tried to push away thoughts of Amersfoort, Nozipho, the shack, the barns, and home back in Nyanga. He stood in reality. His reality.

One evening, Gabriel crouched behind a stack of crates near Mama Chilli's shebeen. He saw men moving in a flash, hands full of boxes. In split seconds, they slipped between the shops and jumped into idling cars. Then they sped off. He froze, awestruck. He had seen scenes like this in movies. He loved Mzansi soapies and could binge them all weekend back home in Nyanga. Watching them had taught him enough to understand why such scoundrels weren't arrested and kept coming back. He spent the whole week studying their pattern.

He found a job.

He started small: picking pockets in shebeens and at the mall. He snatched bags as he figured women were careless. He always acted fast. Brisk, clean, calculated moves. Gabriel told himself it was temporary, that he had no choice. His meagre savings dwindled. Hunger gnawed at him, and with no job in sight, the streets offered an easy way to survive. He had to do what he had to do.

Weeks passed, and the line between survival and crime blurred. He still talked to his friends, yet he never told them he was a thief. He maintained the lie that he owned a spaza shop. People judged too much. They would never understand him. Besides, many people end up in jail for crimes they never intended to commit. Situations can push you into taking steps you never imagined. Life happens.

The dire state of affairs had pushed the three friends from their homes. South Africa's seemingly better fortunes pulled them. That courageous move had been a gamble. Leaving home under uncertain circumstances was never easy.

Meanwhile, in Amersfoort, Farai and Takudzwa accepted that their friend wasn't returning. They missed his carefree sometimes rude nature. Work continued under the same harsh conditions. Each day, they dragged their feet to the fields, dreading another dose of oppression. They figured it was better to fall into the hands of Home Affairs than face the foreman and boss. The police would round them up and cram them into a bus, *Gumbakumba* bus, and take them to the Beitbridge border. There, they would wait until midnight and then cross back. A few rands could get you back into Musina, South Africa side; only the unlucky ones were jailed and not deported.

This game of hide-and-seek was far easier than confronting that ruthless foreman. A fellow Zimbabwean inflicting maximum pain on his countrymen. An advocate for exploitation. All for the love of money, protection and small favours. For how long that would continue, no one knew. Going back to Zimbabwe wasn't an option for them. The reasons why they left were still ongoing. Struggling in South Africa was a better option as they could scrape together enough to buy their own new underwear, a luxury back home.

Farai's girlfriend dumped him after disembarking a commuter omnibus one day. From the backseat to the door, one had to bend. In doing so, his pair of shorts slipped down, revealing his bum crack and tattered briefs. Fellow passengers laughed, muttering comments to each other. The conductor went hysterical, yelling that Farai wore classy jeans and a sweater, but underneath he was all skin. Everyone found it funnier because the whole time he spoke English, sounding fancy, but his Tommy Hilfiger briefs were shredded. Only the waistband remained, along with a few strings of fabric. His girlfriend stormed off, eyes blazing. Children these days. Young love.

It was one of the reasons Farai decided to leave the country: to find work, better himself, and make sure no girl ever treated him like that again. He wanted the good life too. He hadn't gone to school to roam the streets, embarrassing himself on public transport. He hoped to buy a car one day, and as many briefs as he could afford. He swore he'd never wear second-hand briefs again. He'd rather go commando.

Chapter 18

Six months in Manchester, and the city still smelt foreign — damp streets, exhaust fumes, and smoke from a nearby pub. September rains blurred the streetlights, tiny puddles rippling like silver mirrors. Rushed footsteps splashed through the drizzle. The night was always young in the city. The rain tapped the window in a staccato rhythm, coaxing Nancy to sleep. But she had to prepare for work. Overnight shift.

In the tiny flat she shared with Sharon and Rudo, Nancy hunched over a plate of pap dotted with mopane worms. The radiator hissed, warming only a corner of the room, while rain rattled against the single window. Voices rose from the street: shouting, laughter, the clatter of late-night deliveries. Nancy swallowed, grimacing at the chewy worms, and forced a smile. She already craved her Zimbabwean delicacies and Facebook Marketplace had hooked her up with a supplier. Eating mopane worms eased her homesickness.

Thinking about work made her feel sick. She clutched her mouth and ran to the toilet, nausea twisting her stomach. She still struggled to keep up with the visceral images she sometimes encountered at work. Both her friends tolerated work. Nancy kept a straight face, braving it for fear of losing her job. She could stomach baby poop — her own, maybe, but other people's, day after day? That was too much for her. But what other work could she do? The conditions of her Certificate of Sponsorship (CoS) required her to follow certain rules, otherwise, she would have quit on her first day.

Residential aged care was nothing like the hotel she had worked in back home. There, her days had revolved around crisp Egyptian cotton sheets, fragrant towels, and cheerful smiles from guests who barely noticed her. She had received tips, but now she had to work hard to keep her psyche intact. Here, she scrubbed floors every day, helped clients shower, and changed adult diapers. Sometimes cheeky clients harassed her, slurring abuses whether she had made a mistake or not.

The first time she cleaned up after someone, she nearly fainted: the stench from a client, who kept soiled diapers and shorts in a backpack next to his bed, and the helplessness in the old man's eyes. She felt both sorry and disgusted. All in a day's work. She was there for the money; otherwise, her sponsor would alert the United Kingdom Home Office and have her deported.

Sharon, who had organised the CoS's, nudged her one night.

"You'll get it my Nancy," she whispered, giving her a perk on the cheek.

Out here, you had to watch out for one another, otherwise it took a split second to lose your sanity. Rudo, the detective's sister and sharper of the two, had already started cooking Zimbabwean meals in their flat to sell to in WhatsApp groups and channels, stretching her meagre pounds to handle constant calls from family. Countless calls: money, updates, and enough emotional blackmail to drive her mad.

Nancy kept a straight face, muttering under her breath that she'd need a diploma in diplomacy just to survive the calls. Every day was a balancing act: survive the long, draining shifts, keep her mind intact, and somehow stretch every pound to meet obligations from home. Basking in the sun was a luxury she yearned for. Yet, others lounged in the sun, sipping fruit juice, while she worked her ass off. If she bought herself an ice-cream, she celebrated. Bills always knocked at the door.

And then, there was the work itself: scrubbing floors, bathing clients, cleaning their buttholes, changing diapers, cleaning vomit... you name it. All the things she had never imagined herself doing in this lifetime — or any to come. Never say never, indeed. Nothing here resembled the hotel she had once served with a smile. She had to let her heart do the work, not her mind. Thinking about it made her scowl and lose her appetite. She now had to take ginger capsules to stop the nausea before going to work. Life always found a way to humble people.

While Nancy adapted to her new life away from the glitz and glamour of hotel work, another migrant, Gabriel, down in South Africa, acted with a questionable survival instinct. Nancy had once seen him on a video online — documenting his life in South Africa on TikTok. He had grown up understanding the raw pressures of life: unemployment, poverty, and family demands. He posted weekly on TikTok to pass the time and inspire others, showing that nothing and no one should stand in the way of your dreams, even if it meant bending the rules.

Rules, in his eyes, were meant to be broken. Without going into detail about his day-to-day life, Gabriel had said on TikTok that some people turned to prostitution or theft as a way of coping with a world that expected too much from them. People placed ridiculous and unrealistic expectations on others, whether out of entitlement or indebtedness, it was never fair. Watching him, Nancy felt a mixture of awe and unease; she knew the danger, but also the desperation that drove him. That cruel charm was attractive, yet she couldn't help feeling sorry for him too.

In Manchester, Nancy sometimes wondered if she and Gabriel were really different. Both had left home to find opportunities, to send money back home, and above all, to build a better life. To survive. One through work she had never imagined in her wildest nightmares, bathing strangers, cleaning up after them, enduring the humiliation of verbal abuses and physical aggression. The other, through crime, precise and calculated, moving from one victim to another, stealing anything he thought valuable.

As the three friends got busier schedules, Nancy's nights were quieter. Loneliness gnawed at her, a deep longing for a man. She scrolled through Facebook groups, seeking companionship, not a fling. At 26, she was ripe enough to settle. At work, all she did was work and go home. On the buses, or when they hung out on weekends, no one ever approached them.

Meanwhile, Gabriel, in Ermelo, South Africa, had established himself in his own part of the street. He thrived in crowded areas and isolated, bushy paths, opportunistic as ever. Always on the hunt. A bird of prey. Sharp as an eagle. He had long since forgotten about his departed Nozipho. He indulged in one-night stands whenever the urge struck. He hated wasting money on women, but when he did, he splashed it. After all, he risked his ass every day; he deserved to spend his money whichever way he wanted. Still, his family's expectations back home followed him everywhere. On most days he ignored their calls, blue ticking messages depending on his mood. He knew he could never solve the whole clan's problems, though. You can never forget your roots, no matter how wayward you become.

Chapter 19

By the end of her probationary period, Nancy could shower a client without flinching and feed someone with dignity. She could even smile through awkward mealtime incidents.

Together with her two friends, they laughed over work issues, social media buzz, bus schedules, and financial dilemmas. They were all happy to send money home, but they couldn't stand being expected to spend their entire salaries on others. The same people would one day ask, "What good is going to the UK, only to end up with a suitcase of Guccis and LVs?"

Rudo's home-cooked meal delivery business expanded so much that she couldn't keep up with orders. She had to change her business model. She also needed time to rest and have a social life. She now only cooked on weekends, and customers could freeze the food if they wanted. Sharon continued to be the strong-willed one, making fewer complaints but still grumbling now and then. Her level of tolerance appeared to be high. Some people burn inside while keeping a face. When they break down, they break forever.

Nancy had grown stronger and more capable. But one rainy Sunday evening, on her way from work, a drunk passenger stumbled into her on the tram, twisting her ankle. It was minor, but painful enough to leave a small limp. She couldn't afford a day off. Gritting her teeth, she went home, ignoring the throbbing pain. Once there, she narrated her ordeal to her friends, who urged her to rest for a few days. She brushed them off and placed a cold pack on her ankle. She had a shift at 6.30am. Only admission into hospital could stop her. She would hop on the tram again. Money came first. Her people had their eyes on her for allowances and upkeep, let alone her own needs.

As Nancy tried to sleep, her phone kept buzzing. Three WhatsApp missed calls and one from Facebook Messenger; all from her pastor in Zimbabwe. She had messaged him about her minor incident. When the calls stopped, a short message popped up, instructing her to seed US$300 to stop further attacks. An additional US$100 would unleash next level blessings for promotion at work. After reading, she blocked and deleted his number. Bullshit!

Ten years of loyalty to his church gone in ten seconds. Nonsense. Absolute nonsense. When she was in Zimbabwe no one in that church paid any attention to her. During the Covid-19 lockdowns she begged for help, food, anything, but no one chipped in. The time she caught malaria on her first trip to Mt Darwin, not a single person checked on her. Now, they heard she was in the diaspora, and suddenly they all had her number on speed-dial.

Nancy scrunched her face and mimicked his tone, "My daughter... my foot." With all the toiling she endured, he had the nerve. She sulked and switched her phone off.

Her friends roared in laughter. Sharon had never believed in those so-called prophets and apostles who claimed they could "release blessings" over their congregants. Most of them survived by preying on church members overseas. Being abroad was hard enough. Endless legal fees, nonstop paperwork, documents that always needed paying, and everything came with a massive price tag. In her first week in the UK, she told one pastor to keep her share of blessings and use them to improve his own life, since he seemed to be distributing them from a personal stash.

Rudo even added that she had seen people from overseas receiving VIP treatment in church, front-row seats, reserved parking and mineral water to hype them into sowing seeds. Of course, the men of cloth always reap where they never sow, only where they see money. Church should be about love for all people, not lust for money.

Laughter, indeed, was the best medicine. That good, hearty laugh after blocking the cunning pastor relieved some of Nancy's pain, though her ankle had swollen. In her sleep, she whimpered and writhed, whispering Simon's name.

"Simon... yes, Simon," she murmured over and over, her voice trailing off into the night.

Under the warm glow of an LED lamp on the bedside table, Sharon nudged Rudo, eyebrows raised, eyes wide. Their heads tilted toward Nancy. She slept on, drooling. She had never mentioned a Simon. Who was he, and why was Nancy calling his name in her sleep?

Chapter 20

After long shifts at the aged care home, the three women often sat on the narrow balcony of their flat, the city lights of Manchester glowing on the streets below. Each busied herself with her phone, EarPods in. Dinner time meant phones away, but Nancy's fingers hovered over hers, scrolling through Facebook groups for immigrants and Zimbabwean communities. Names; faces, messages, videos, she clicked through them all with a mixture of frowns and chuckles.

Nancy had always kept herself busy, moving through the days in a haze of work shifts, errands, and long nights scrolling through Facebook groups. Time and again, Sharon gave her perks on the cheek. Sometimes Nancy recalled that kiss when that jerk called Jeff played her. That womaniser almost ruined her feelings for men. She'd long since got over him, and now they could even joke about it.

Even though she now talked less with her friends, they spent quality time together on weekends. Living together wasn't the hard part, work was. Long shifts, late nights, early mornings, and they were usually too tired to sit around and chat during the week. On weekends, they only left their cosy flat for something worth going out for. Otherwise, they stayed in and watched movies on their cobalt-blue Victoria couch. Sharon usually volunteered to cook, as long as she didn't have to wash the dishes. Nancy didn't mind; she liked cleaning the house. Rudo handled the groceries and took all their laundry to the launderette. Sometimes they got on each other's nerves, but they had long established healthy space and boundaries. That way, their friendship flourished.

One thing was certain, they all missed home. Nancy missed the dusty streets of Epworth on the eastern outskirts of Harare, and the petrichor, that musky, rainy smell that always reminded her of her first love in the tuckshop. She would lean through the counter slot to kiss him as the rain drizzled outside. The naivety of youth. In Manchester, her heart skipped when she found a perfume called Petrichor. That earthy scent of rain and damp streets gave her goosebumps, a fragment of home, a memory of rain-soaked streets and her first kiss. She pictured potholes filled with water, the scent of wet dust mingling with roasted mealie cobs at the corner, while neighbours leaned over fences, chatting and laughing. Children waded through the puddles, splashing without a care, while their mothers ran after them, scolding them for trying to catch bilharzia in the dirty water. She reminisced about the familiar shouts of street vendors, the touts whistling for commuters, and the commuter omnibus drivers revving their engines to entice passengers. That rhythm of everyday life made Epworth feel like home. The pulse of her ghetto. Now, there was no neighbour to call out to. They were stuck in their cramped apartment, decent enough to give them a good night's sleep. They say home is where the heart is. But sometimes, the heart longs for another heart.

Nancy also missed the familiar faces on her walk to the bus stop. She missed the airy hotel in Victoria Falls where she had worked. She'd never slept on a single bed before arriving in the UK. None of them had. They promised themselves a bigger flat once they could afford it. In the meantime, they had to strike a balance between their own needs with those of the people back home. Necessity over comfort. On those single beds, loneliness crept in. Social media helped, but Rudo preferred books from thrift stores or she read on her Kindle. Sharon teased her about being addicted to Facebook, claiming it was why she acted "ghetto."

All Nancy wanted was to find love, no man had ever approached her on the streets. She imagined laughter echoing through the streets she once walked. She remembered the thrill of standing on the street, chatting for hours, a habit she had broken when she moved to work in Victoria Falls. Even in her dreams, she was back there on the dusty streets of Epworth, rain dripping on her face. Back at the tuckshop, leaning across the counter, feeling the warmth of that first kiss. It was an imprint that stayed with her forever.

The memories of Epworth always clung to her, but life in Manchester didn't wait, and she often felt she couldn't keep up. She often returned from work drained, wishing for companionship. Not that her friends weren't enough. She longed for that one person to send her good morning messages, someone to exchange sweet nothings with. To fill the gap, Nancy scrolled through social media more often than she wanted to admit. That was why Sharon had always teased her about being addicted to Facebook. An unhealthy pastime, she'd say. Rudo would jump in too, claiming Facebook suited her because it was "the ghetto of social media. Let her be". It was Nancy's way of coping with homesickness, of missing her ghetto.

It was on one of social media life coach's pages that she first came across Simon. People submitted questions to the coach's inbox every day, often requesting to be posted as anonymous. Others used ghost accounts. They sought advice in the comments, but one message caught her eye. A Zimbabwean man was looking for a woman to marry, between twenty-five and forty-five. Someone who didn't care about size. He lived in Poland and claimed he was ready to marry. He promised he would never ask for nudes, unlike what others were doing, and that he would be following the comments section to cherry pick.

Nancy lingered on the post, reading and rereading it, curiosity prickling at her. Who was this man? And why did she feel an unexpected pull toward his words? She had only written "Good luck." Then the person behind the post slid into her direct mails (DMs). She ignored the message for a week, though her heart throbbed to know more about him. Conversations about size dominated across the globe, online, in chats, and in whispered discussions. The obsession was on steroids. But since when did size matter for love or marriage? Since when had superficial preferences become a requirement for marriage? No wonder divorce rates kept climbing. A depraved generation. Marriage was supposed to be about the inner person.

By the second week, Nancy messaged him every day. She liked what she saw. They messaged cautiously at first, short messages, jokes about missing home, little bits of small talk about life abroad. Then a rhythm took shape: late-night texts that dragged on, filled with laughter, sighs, and the occasional shared screenshot from social media. They exchanged frustrations about work and home, celebrated tiny victories, and whispered their dreams and aspirations on voice notes. It wasn't much, texts and emojis, but each message made her smile and warmed her up.

Nancy felt less alone, as if the distance between them shrank with each conversation. When they moved to the sweet-nothings, Nancy still kept her relationship hidden from her friends. Simon, on the other hand, shared everything with his friends in South Africa — Farai, Gabriel and Takudzwa. He was no longer the Simon who had chickened out of their illegal border crossing into South Africa. No longer a coward. The faint-hearted never achieved anything in life. He was a man now. A man out to make money at any cost. For too long, he had watched the few privileged amass wealth. Enough.

Chapter 21

With Christmas approaching, Gabriel moved to Joburg. It had already been eight months since they'd moved to South Africa, and he knew his lifestyle needed to match his hard work. Even his friends, Farai and Takudzwa, had left the farms and made their way to Joburg. He, too, had adapted, earning enough from theft to afford a small studio apartment. He had to enjoy the bloody fruits of his labour.

Every day, he gambled with his life, putting his neck on the line to feed himself. The days of eating pilchards for dinner were over. The small, oily fish in a can, enough to fill the stomach, under ten rand. No more scraping by. He came first now. No more prioritising others—people who enjoyed sweet dreams while he lay awake with one eye open like a dog.

Gabriel's decision to move to Joburg stemmed from the rising tension between the police, the locals, and foreigners. Hostility against African foreigners was growing, and he figured he might as well move to the big city, maximise his trade, and plan an exit strategy. He'd rather be arrested for stealing a million than a thousand. Even in Joburg, police sirens, neighbourhood gossip, and rival thieves made every move risky. But he had learned to adapt: a flash of movement and careful calculation. He was now fully entrenched in a life that had once horrified him, but necessity had rewritten morality.

Diaspora life could push one to one's limits. Family pressures, unpaid school fees for cousins, and constant calls from home pushed him deeper into crime. The only people he owed were his maternal grandparents, who had raised him after he was orphaned at nine. For everyone else, it was out of his generosity and mood. He lived on adrenaline, always on flight mode, and used his money as he pleased, without feeling guilty. All the bullshit emotional blackmail could wait.

The streets of Johannesburg were no longer plain dangerous; they were hostile. The whispers, the stares in taxis, and the casual insults from neighbours; he saw it everywhere. Each encounter reminded him that, as a migrant, he was never truly welcome. Xenophobia crept into every interaction. The way people looked away when he spoke. The stares that followed him down the street. The comments that branded him an outsider. It left him raw and drove him to steal more. It is difficult to fully understand the mind of a criminal.

At first, he tried to work honestly, taking temporary jobs at traffic lights whenever he could. But he never stayed long. He struggled to fight the strong urge to steal. His employers doubted him and continued to pass subtle threats. Even the children on the streets sneered at any Mukwerekwere. Worse still, the police descended on the streets, conducting random raids.

He upgraded his game, moving faster, taking riskier decisions. Small thefts became organised, methodical, and calculated. He studied patterns among other Zimbabwean and Malawian thieves. He learnt who to trust and who to avoid, and bit by bit, he became a professional in his own right. By the time he vanished into the night with boxes stuffed into his white Volkswagen Golf, he was thriving in the only way the world seemed to allow him. They erased the idea of morality. No one cared about anyone, why would he.

Across the ocean in Manchester, news of regulatory upheaval sent shockwaves through social media. On the small TV in the girls' flat, a reporter spoke of tightening work visa rules for all migrants, of hospitals and care homes, and of increasing scrutiny on anyone seeking to stay in the UK. The effects of Brexit were still being felt, as workers from countries like Estonia, once able to come and go freely, now faced red tape and uncertainty, like other non-EU citizens.

Nancy swallowed hard. Her CoS had secured her job, but with every new policy announcement and headline, her future in the diaspora became more fragile by the day. Even her friends were struggling with this development. Losing their CoS every time a new law came into effect, made them more anxious, unsure of what might happen next. If someone flawed like Kemi Badenoch, with her views on race and immigration could rise so high in British politics, what hope did they have? Legal migrants, trying their best to follow the rules, were left questioning where they stood. The system seemed to reward those who didn't even bother to integrate.

At work, Nancy noticed how her colleagues whispered the new policies, and how managers talked in hushed tones about compliance and inspections. Even the smallest mistake could trigger paperwork nightmares. Everyone now walked on eggshells. It was exhausting for Nancy, her competence always under scrutiny, her life shaped as much by the law as by her skills.

Meanwhile, across continents in South Africa, xenophobia had gone national, fuelled by politics and media coverage. Rumours of crackdowns on foreigners, stricter policing in migrant-heavy neighbourhoods, and sensationalised news reports made the streets even more hostile. Gabriel had to be swifter, plan smarter, and avoid the police, who seemed to patrol with bias, targeting migrants like him. Gabriel tuned into global debates on migration, economic inequality, and crime through podcasts on YouTube and WhatsApp channels. Discussions within the African Union (AU) and Southern African Development Community (SADC) sparked debates among migrants and locals alike. Gabriel soon realised that, whether in cities or villages, survival demanded more than endurance; it required agility and cunning.

Chapter 22

Sharon was a strong character, for no challenge seemed too big for her. she had prepared to move to the UK and was determined to make it by any means necessary. Upon arrival, she met a former classmate from Grade Three to Form Six, John Dube, whom she lived with in the same street in Mabvuku, Harare.They had known each other from the time they were learning at Kurai Primary School during the time of the great Joseph B Kaseke—a prodigious leader and disciplinarian par excellence.

When Sharon spoke to her mother about meeting John, she was excited, believing that her daughter had finally found someone she knew, someone who was going to handhold her and show her around the UK, until she settled. John started by sending small gifts every Saturday morning. Occasionally, he would take her to the movies. However, there was always a mystery over his life. Questions were always lingering: Was he married? How about children? Was he interested in her, and if so, how was it going to work? They had last seen each other many years ago.

One Monday evening, Sharon retrieved her phone and there were ten missed calls from John. Too tired to return the calls, she went to bed. The following morning, she was starting work at 9am. By 8am, there had been 15 missed calls from him.

Sharon decided to talk to Nancy about the matter later that day. Before 10am, she had received a bouquet of flowers, Ferrero chocolates and a note.

"Hey, beautiful; I have been thinking about you. I have been calling you and when you did not pick up, I got worried. Please let me know if you are well. Return my call as soon as you can; I am unsettled," the note read.

Sharon wanted to take the matter casually. However, after confiding in Nancy, she was advised to keep a record of all their communication. Her friend had a sixth sense, which turned out right in most cases.

"Nancy dearest, I have been receiving calls from John nonstop. Last night I missed ten of his calls owing to my shift, imagine! Do you think it's normal, or I'm just fretting over nothing? Sharon asked.

Nancy looked her friend straight in the eye for a while the way a criminal investigator does. And when she spoke, her voice was deliberately slow, firm and authoritative.

"Well, how long have you known him?" She asked.

Sharon was unsure of what to say. Yes, she had known John since primary school, but there was a yawning gap in their communication, which somehow sapped her of confidence.

In the end, she could only say: "I have known him in the past when we were young but so many years have gone by since then. We only reconnected here in the UK."

The gravity of the matter weighed heavily on her, as evidenced in the way she gasped for air.

As if transfixed on the spot—not blinking—not moving, Nancy stared at her blankly, devoid of words. Her silence echoed. Yet, even as she finally regained speech, words were no longer necessary. Sharon had gotten the message loud and clear.

"Sharon, you should be careful here. This is not Zimbabwe. If you play it the Zimbabwean way here, you will rue the day you landed at Heathrow Airport. We're in a jungle here, where there is neither friend nor family; only survival. You're on your own, my dear, so, there is no good reason to trust anybody. There is no middle ground—nothing—except you. Learn that fast or perish! she ranted, adding, "This Ubuntu/Hunhu philosophy is for Africa and not Europe. This is England; wake up!"

Nancy's candid words hit like a thousand packed punches, fracturing her gut, bruising her ego and breaking her soul.

Smarting from the honesty and sisterly concern in her friend's words, that afternoon at lunchtime, Sharon called John.

"Hello John! How have you been? Thank you for the flowers and the note. I am so grateful for your thoughtfulness. You really didn't have to do that at all," Sharon said.

"Ooh, Sharon; I am so glad to hear from you. I was getting worried. As for the flowers, you shouldn't mention, knowing how far we have come. I hope you liked them", John responded, encouraged.

"One other thing," John said, as an afterthought, "I wanted to share something with you if you have time."

"Johnny boy; you scare me when you talk like that, hey. What is it now? Am I in trouble? Are you ok?" Sharon asked.

"Since childhood, this feeling has been eluding words. I always felt it but I couldn't muster the courage to tell you. The thing is," John hesitated, and finally said, "I think I am in love with you."

"Johnny, you surprise me! Why now? Why here? Just reflect on this: you are a married man and have children here in the United Kingdom. You don't need any extra burden; you should focus on your family," Sharon said firmly.

At least she is worried about her being an extra burden on me. She is not rejecting me outright, John thought out loud. But Nancy meant every word and heard him.

Unsure of how to proceed, he paused momentarily, then fumed:

"You know, I am not really sure what you mean by that. I have done a lot for you, and treated you fine. Is that how you treat me?"

He terminated the call, leaving Sharon in shock. It didn't surprise her, though. It was common for people to have high school fantasies carried through to adulthood. Nonetheless, suggesting that the few items he bought her were worth of her consideration of him was unthinkable.

The night following the call, and just before she retired to bed, Sharon's phone buzzed. It was a Zimbabwean number. She ignored it, taking it for one of those SOS calls from home. She went to sleep, but when she woke up to pee, there were thirty-five missed call alerts and twenty-two WhatsApp messages on her mobile.

Anxiously, she sat on the couch and opened the messages. Blinded by the phone light, she used one eye to read as the other adjusted.

"Sharon, your Facebook account has been hacked. There are nude pictures on your page; and we have been trying to get in touch with you," A message from Lizzy read.

She opened another one. Maxwell's read, "Sharon, there is a John who claims that you borrowed money from him to pay for your visa; and that you are refusing to pay back. He claims that you are now offering to pay in kind—through sex."

There was a particular aunt whom Sharon never got along with since childhood. She often complained about her to her siblings and other relatives over the phone and chat groups. The audios were posted on WhatsApp family groups and relations immediately soured.

Anna, one of her classmates in high school, said: "Hey love. I would like to let you know that there is a nigger claiming you have been getting money to support your parents back home from him, and now you're refusing to pay back. Please report the bagger to the police; he deserves to be locked up."

Sharon was heartbroken. She called her employer at once and the matter was reported to the police. It took three hours for the

Manchester Metropolitan Police to record all the details of the alleged stalking.

Chief Superintendent Macmillan Griffiths was in charge of the department overseeing the stalking and harassment cases. He was a man of very few words and many questions.

"Madam Sharon, tell me, how do you know the suspect?" Chief Supt Griffiths asked casually as if discussing an unimportant matter.

Sharon was not too sure how to respond. In the end, she said, "From childhood."

Chief Supt Griffiths jotted something and gazed at her inquisitively.

"How did you interact with him? Was it same neighbourhood, school or church?" he continued.

Sharon reflected: "We have known each other back in Zimbabwe from lower primary school and attended the same high school up to the sixth form. We went to the same church, and at school, we were in the choir and same social club."

The investigating officer took notes for some time, then asked politely: "Did you share any intimate feelings before coming to the UK?"

"Not really. I recall that during our time in the school choir, we practiced together on weekends and shared the same bench. We were great friends, but not in an intimate way," answered. .

"Have you acted in any manner that showed that you were interested in him but you were waiting for him to ask?" Chief Supt Griffiths enquired.

"No."

"Do you love him?"

Sharon paused, as she hadn't really asked herself how she felt about John.,

"No," she said plainly.

"Have you ever made any request for money from the suspect?" Chief Supt Griffiths asked.

"I have never asked for any assistance from him. Whatever he did for me was of his own volition. And it was always small gifts", she replied.

The questioning went on for about three hours, and her cautioned statement was recorded. A docket was opened against John.

The following morning, John called her three times but she rebuffed him.. He even bombarded her with text and WhatsApp messages, which were ignored as well. Frustrated, he switched on his television set and tuned it to a news station. Just about that time, there was a light knock on the main door. A feminine scent wafted in as he opened the door. He froze.

It was Sharon, all right. And behind her were two uniformed stern looking policemen.

"Good day, sir! Do you by any chance answer to the name John? the taller one asked politely.

"Yes, sir", John stammered.

"I am afraid, sir, you're under arrest for suspected stalking of Ms Sharon Tapfuma, causing discomfort and disturbing her peace as well as criminal nuisance. May you please accompany us to the police station? Remember, whatever you say from this moment may be used against you in a court of law," the policeman said, respectfully but authoritatively.

In no time, John was hauled to the parked police vehicle, handcuffed. He was barred from communicating with Sharon, either directly or through proxies.

Chapter 23

John was held at Manchester Metropolitan Police Station waiting to go to the Magistrates' Court. The UK law, just like elsewhere around the world, restrict the number of hours a person can be held without a bail.

This practice is rooted in English common law with the Magna Carta (1215), solidified by the writ of habeas corpus, and championed globally by jurists like Luis Kutner, who pushed for a UN version after World War II, leading to protections in the Universal Declaration of Human Rights (UDHR) and subsequent international law.

The matter was sat for on a Thursday morning, with Her Worship Elizabeth Wayford presiding.

"All rise," a clerk of court announced as she entered the courtroom.

All in the gallery bowed and remained standing till she sat down. She gesticulated for them to take their seats.

Magistrate Wayford was of Irish American origin. She was elegantly dressed in a black suit and white shirt, regally draped over in a magisterial gown. She placed her gavel lightly on the polished desk, looked sternly at the dock and scanned the gallery. She was firm and friendly and had a success rate of more than eighty-nine percent. Her judgments were rarely overturned by higher courts.

"Good morning, Lesly, what do we have here?" She said gently, conversing with the clerk of court.

"Your Worship, we have State versus John Dube, a case of suspected stalking and harassment," Lesly responded immediately.

The prisons officer, Sergeant Mike Thompson, was a firm wide-eyed tall man of athletic built. He was known for manhandling anyone who entertained thoughts of disrupting court proceedings. He was also responsible for whisking away convicted persons.

"Who is here for the state?" the magistrate asked.

"A man in his early forties stood up, fast and swift, holding some files. His name was Jacob Minfiled. While his name seemed odd, he was, indeed, a minefield in prosecuting cases, having been at the game for more than twenty years.

Simon Northwood, a barrister, defended.

"May the accused, please rise," the magistrate said. "State your name for the record."

"My name is John Dube," he replied.

After all background checks, the magistrate continued: "John Dube, you are hereby charged with the criminal stalking of one Ms Sharon Tapfuma. Do you understand the charges?" she asked.

"She is a lying motherfucker," John said looking at Sharon who was seated in the witness' section.

"John Dube, I want to warn you that use of foul language is not allowed in my courtroom. Do not try that again. And, please answer the question directly as asked," the magistrate said, visibly annoyed. "Do you understand the charges you are facing."

"Yes, Your Worship," John said, a bit toned down, before ranting again, "That bitch will definitely get what she deserves. I'll sue her ass for all this shit she has put me through."

He said seething with anger and visibly shaking, much to the irritation of Magistrate Wayford. She lifted her gavel and swiftly tapped it on the desk.

"I hereby find you guilty of contempt of court. You're to pay £5 000 in the next two weeks failure of which you will be imprisoned for a period not less than six months. Do you want to try for £10 000?" she asked politely yet sarcastically.

"Your Worship, I am still in shock. I am sorry for the manner in which I have acted," he pleaded.

"Do you understand the charges levelled against you?" the magistrate asked again, impatiently but in a contained tone.

"I haven't committed any offence. Is it possible for me to talk to the complainant privately? I am sure this can be settled out of court," John said, his temper flaring.

The magistrate summoned the defence counsel.

"I am not sure what this is all about, but I have a lot of cases lined up. May you kindly advise the accused to cooperate, otherwise we will reschedule this case for another day," she reprimanded

"I understand the charges," John shouted after overhearing the magistrate talking to his lawyer.

After consulting with the state and clerk of court, the magistrate proclaimed, "Your trial date has been set in three weeks' time. I advise you to apply for bail."

While John was trying to comprehend what had just happened, the mean-looking prisons officer swiftly pounced and led him to a waiting van to take him back to reman prison pending bail application.

That night, there was a television programme and the topic under discussion was "Stalking and Harassment" The Commissioner of Police Timothy Cook was the guest in conversation with Mark Porso. They were joined by Mrs Nicole Benza, a United Kingdom-based psychologist.

"Commissioner Cook, welcome to our programme. Our topic today is Stalking and Harassment," The host opened the conversation.

"Good evening viewers. Thank you for inviting me to this crucial conversation, Mark. It is really an honour for me to be here," the commissioner said in his signature respectful demeanour.

"Are we having a problem here in the UK regarding stalking and harassment or people are sounding false alarm?" Mark asked casually.

"Well to put perspective, Mark, according to the Office for National Statistics (ONS), of all the people who experienced partner abuse in the year ending March 2022, 20,8 percent were once stalked.

"What is more, the Crown Prosecution Service (CPS) stated that between 2019 and 2020, a record 2 228 cases of stalking were tried, more than doubling on the figures recorded five years earlier.
g

Mrs Benza looked at the notes she had been scribbling, and without waiting to be given the floor, joined the discussion: "Stalking is common in our society these days.

"However, the CPS also recognises that this may also be driven by improved recognition of stalking among police as part of a wider domestic abuse pattern. Indeed, a random sample of stalking cases in England and Wales showed that 84 percent of complaints were against ex-partners, with three-quarters of those having previously reported other forms of domestic abuse during the relationship."

"Mrs Benza, perhaps we should have started by defining what exactly constitutes stalking and harassment. How does one know that they are stalking someone and, in the process, committing an offence. Or how do you know that you are being stalked?" Mark asked.

"Thank you Mark, well, that's an important starting point. Stalking refers to a pattern of unwanted and repeated behaviours that make an individual feel afraid or threatened. Victims also describe it as a feeling of being harassed or pestered. It can involve following or watching someone, repeatedly contacting them, turning up at their home or workplace, sending unwanted gifts, sending messages repeatedly, or engaging in any behaviour that can cause fear or distress to the victim.

"Stalking is a crime of persistence. The behaviour experienced by victims often seems inevitable and unescapable, which is why it can have such a damaging effect. While the actions of a stalker may seem relatively banal or even harmless, this is often why so many victims suffer for such prolonged periods before reporting it, or even not report it at all," she explained.

"Wow! That is a mouthful. Coming to you commissioner. So, who does this definition fit in, considering that when you want something from someone you have to be persistent? In the 1990s, when we were growing up, it was common to pursue a girl, send flowers or other gifts, call and repeatedly write her letters until she accepted. Are you saying there is no more courtship and people should not try?"

"Mark, you should understand that those were great times and there were fewer social troubles. People were honest with each other. But that's not the case nowadays Mark. Society has changed drastically. What used to matter in the past, no longer does. Hence, the need to set clear social boundaries as dynamics change," Commissioner Cook elaborated.

"So how do you draw the line between perseverance and stalking?" Mark followed it up.

"I think one has to remain with the confines of the law in whatever they do. The other thing is to find out whether your communication is causing discomfort to other individuals or not. You should ask if the person is okay being called at particular times of the day, or whether the gifts are welcome. Getting frequent feedback may help you assess if you are not taking it too far," the commissioner remarked.

He added: "Police records show that many victims of stalking are stalked for years, with the average case lasting around 15 months. What's more, over thirty percent of people who contacted the National Stalking Helpline reported that they had been stalked for over two years, with thirteen percent reporting it having lasted over five."

"Stalking is a serious crime and can cause significant emotional and psychological harm to the victim. Stalking behaviour must be taken seriously; hence victims are urged to seek help. It can happen to anyone. Former partners, friends or acquaintances, work colleagues, and strangers can all be stalkers."

"Does stalking have categories or types?" Mark continued with his line of questioning.

"Indeed, there are, and these include but are not limited to, physical stalking, cyberstalking, erotomania, obsessional stalking, celebrity stalking, and revenge stalking," the commissioner listed them in quick succession, his eyes fixed at Mrs Benza.

"Physical stalking: this type of stalking is what most people presume it to be. It involves a perpetrator following a victim, waiting for them outside their home or workplace, or showing up in other places that they know their victim frequents, like the gym, park or a relative's house," Mrs Benza weighed in.

"Commissioner, you spoke about cyberstalking , how does this work in this increasingly digitised world?" Mark asked.

"Cyberstalking is sometimes called online stalking. It involves using online methods to stalk a victim. This could be in the form of emails, social media and messaging apps. The stalker may send messages, images or videos to harass, intimidate, threaten or scare the victim. Cyberstalking can include posting defamatory or humiliating content online, spreading false rumours or using online tracking tools to monitor what a victim does. In extreme cases, cyber-stalkers can hack into devices to gain access to a victim's accounts or personal information," Commissioner Cook explained.

" Mrs Benza, there was reference to erotomania. Many of our viewers would like to know what it is. May you please elaborate on that?" Mark asked in a soft steady voice, his gaze focused and intentional.

"Well, erotomania; not many people have heard of it. It is a psychological delusional disorder in which the stalker has a false and persistent belief that their victim is in love with them. Most of the time, their victim is of a higher status, a celebrity or someone in a position of authority.

"The stalker may well believe that their victim is someone sending them secret messages or signals or communicating with them in some way, for example, through gestures or body language.

"Erotomania often leads to stalking behaviour as the individual affected may attempt to contact or pursue the object of their affection in an effort to establish a relationship. This behaviour is quite often dangerous and can cause emotional distress for both the victim and the individual with erotomania," She explained before continuing.

"Celebrity stalking is where a stalker fixates on a celebrity and engages in a persistent and unwanted pursuit of them, far beyond that of a typical superfan. Concerning revenge stalking; this involves stalking someone to get revenge or to 'get back' at someone for a perceived wrongdoing. A revenge stalker seeks retribution for something. It's often driven by a desire to exert control over the victim and to make them feel afraid or vulnerable.

"No matter the kind of stalking, it has a huge impact on the victim and can lead to psychological distress, including anxiety and depression, and even post-traumatic stress disorder (PTSD)."

"Thank you very much, Mrs Benza for such an articulate explanation on the different types of stalking. Our phone-in lines are now open for those with burning questions or experiences to share," Mark said. "Our discussion is on stalking, the telltale signs and how one can tell they're being stalked."

"Hello," answered the first call.

"Hello Mark, how are you? My name is Daniel from London. I want to comment on the question regarding stalking."

"Please go ahead."

"Many people picture stalkers as unknown men hiding in the shadows or a superfan who follows a particular celebrity. However, the truth is, it's much more complex than most people believe.

Regardless of who is doing the stalking, the behaviours demonstrated are often similar.

"The signs of stalking behaviour often involve a pattern of persistent and unwanted behaviours over time," Daniel said, his voice firm and full of conviction, exhibiting probable expertise on the subject.

Another caller going by the name Joe from Leeds joined the discussion:

"The acts are varied but may include following someone, turning up unexpectedly where their victim is, surveillance – watching someone continuously or repeatedly.

"This can include sitting outside a person's house or place of work, Sending repeated unwanted gifts, including flowers or other items, despite the victim requesting that they stop. It also involves monitoring someone's activities online, such as repeatedly checking someone's social media accounts, emails or phone records."

Mark picked another caller named Lizzy from Kent: "Please go ahead with your contribution ma'am."

"Unwanted contact such as receiving repeated phone calls, text messages, emails or other forms of communication from someone, despite not wanting to engage with them, and trespassing. The stalker may enter the victim's property or workplace without permission. What all of these behaviours have in common is that the perpetrator is fixated and obsessed with the victim and their actions are both unwanted yet repeated," Lizzy contributed to the raging discussion.

There were many more people on the phone lines than Mark could handle. Turning to Commissioner Cook, he said: "Please tell us, what are the warning signs that someone is stalking you?"

"The four warning signs of stalking, which summarise the behaviour are:

F - Fixated

O - Obsessive

U – Unwanted

R – Repeated."

"That is profound commissioner," Mark commented.

"In your view, Mrs Benza; who is at risk of being stalked?

"Well, according to a stalking charity, the Suzy Lamplugh Trust, for about forty-five percent of those who contact their stalking helpline, their stalker is an ex-partner. Aside from those, a further third of the victims say they have previously known their stalker in some way, perhaps even just as a brief encounter.

"This means that anyone can be a victim of stalking. Dr Lorraine Sheridan's report for the Network for Surviving Stalking found that the stalking victims surveyed were between ten and seventy-three years of age. Both men and women were affected and victims were from the whole socioeconomic spectrum.

"Indeed, thirty-eight percent of victims classed themselves as professionals. As Dr Sheridan concluded, almost anyone can be a victim of stalking. The only way of avoiding it would be turning to a social recluse," Mrs Benza said.

She added: "Anyone can be a stalker. Anyone can be stalked.

"Having said that, there are some things which may increase a person's risk of being stalked.

"These include sex. Women are more likely to be victims than men. According to the Office for National Statistics, the March 2016 Crime Survey for England and Wales (CSEW) showed that across all the sub-categories of intimate violence, estimates for women were statistically significantly higher than those for men. At least 20,9 percent of women had experienced stalking since the age of 16 compared with 9,9 percent for men.

"Age also plays a part. The same CSEW survey showed that women aged between sixteen and nineteen, constituting 19,7 percent, and twenty to twenty-four, representing 6,6 percent, were more likely to be victims of stalking than women in other age groups. The same trend was noted in male victims of stalking, 4,2 percent and 4,4 percent in the corresponding age categories, respectively.

Another category is single and divorced adults: Stalkers are often ex-partners or former acquaintances who are unable to let go of the relationship and become obsessed with their victim. The CSEW survey showed that this is the case for both men and women.

Then, occupation in which people in certain professions may well be at higher risk of being stalked due to the nature of their roles. This may include law enforcement, social workers, or those who work in public offices.

Also, people who post a lot on social media, especially in a public way and share personal information, may be more at risk of becoming victims of stalking behaviours than those who refrain and are more private.

"Concerning geographical location, those who live in cities or densely populated areas and engage in public activities may be more at risk than those who live in rural areas.

"Finally, celebrities or public figures are at much more risk of being stalked due to their public presence. They are particularly vulnerable to erotomania."

"Mrs Benza, we are running out of time. In under a minute, can you tell us what causes stalking behaviour?" Mark asked.

"Mark, it's tough to explain in one minute, but I will try. Essentially, stalking is caused by a wish to exert control. What drives that desire is often complex. Each stalker will have a unique underlying socio-cognitive model, which drives them to their actions and feelings. Overall, stalking behaviour appears to come from obsessive thinking and something called 'relatedness'," she explained, almost out of breath and sliding towards the edge of her seat.

Stealing a glance at Mark and judging his enthusiasm, she decided to slip in a few more words, even though the minute had lapsed.

"Relatedness is an elementary psychological need for belonging and connection. It is possible, therefore, that stalking behaviours emerge from this overrunning desire for connection that has somehow been thwarted.

"In conclusion, psychologists believe that stalking may come from a combination of thwarted relatedness with negative fantasies. Negative fantasies, as opposed to positive ones with, which we're more familiar, are those where a person fantasises about negative experiences such as loss or imagining a partner leaving."

She lowered the microphone, slouched in her chair and adjusted posture into a relaxed mode.

"Mrs Benza, you may want to comment on ex-lovers in a minute?" Commission Cook quipped, taking Mark by surprise.

"I thought I am the chair here, but what can one do to a commissioner? Mark said defeatedly

Mrs Benza explained: "It has been established that those who may have endured past abusive romantic relationships are often vulnerable to stalking from their ex-partners.

"It can emerge from the termination of a romantic relationship whereby a perpetrator wants to win their former partner back or ward off any potential new love interests. This kind of stalking is driven by a dependency known as 'relationship contingent self-esteem'. This means the individual only sees their worth via the relationship, therefore, they respond with intense jealousy and anger when that relationship breaks down. This can lead to the obsessive pursuit of their former partner."

As a remand prisoner, John was legally presumed innocent until proven guilty. Unlike convicted criminals, he was allowed to wear his own clothes, watch an in-cell TV, receive regular visits, and use the phone while he awaited his trial.

Chapter 24

It was a Thursday morning, three weeks after John's initial appearance in court, when Her Worship Elizabeth Wayford sat in her high leather chair, gazing at everyone in the courtroom through bespectacled eyes. After consultations and background discussions with the clerk of court in low tones, she finally looked up.

"We are here to hear the bail application for John Dube in a case of suspected stalking and harassment," she said.

The state was represented by Jacob Minfiled, while Simon Northwood represented the accused.

"Your Worship, you have been one of the finest advocates for justice in all England. Your quest for justice and dedication to truth has been unparalleled. You've symbolically stood for justice, and-" Northwood went lyrical.

"Your Worship, are we in a serious court of law or what?" Counsellor Minfiled protested.

"Stay on point counsellor," Her Worship insisted in a firm voice.

"Your Worship, we have one prayer before this honourable court. We seek the release on bail of the accused on the basis that he has the right to be treated as innocent until proven guilty beyond reasonable doubt by a competent court of law. In our modern justice delivery system, even the accused have rights that must be upheld. We therefore, seek the unconditional release on bail of John Dube." Northwood prayed.

The magistrate took notes as she waited for the state to respond.

"Your Worship, our team travelled to Zimbabwe to gather facts about the accused. The accused entered the UK under the pretext that he was seeking asylum as the ruling party in Zimbabwe wanted to kill him. However, no evidence proved that he had any political or business interests warranting reason for political persecution," Minfiled said.

"Records from the Financial Clearing Bureau, the FCB, an institution responsible for clearing those with a financial record, showed that the accused had multiple borrowings from three banks and accounts with clothing retailers that he never settled.

"It turned out that he was yoked by debt and took advantage of our friendly laws and abundant generosity. Everything he submitted to Immigration was false, hence his citizenship must be nullified.

"At the age of eighteen, he was accused of sodomising a 17-year-old boy. The case crumbled as the minor's parents withdrew the case under unclear circumstances. He was also charged with rape, and again, the complainant skipped court. She never testified in court. She was found dead and postmortem results revealed that death was due to poisoning, although there were indications of bruising on her body and other signs consistent with strangling. Either threats on the person of the pathologist or corruption can only be reasonable pointers to why death by suicide was preferred. Turning to-," Minfiled's train of events was interrupted.

"Objection Your Worship," Northwood protested.

"On what basis, counsellor?" Magistrate Wayford asked.

"Leading, Your Worship. These are old women's tales; bedtime stories with no concrete evidence or strong basis on the matter. The insinuation that the accused is a criminal does not hold water since he was never convicted. Any accusation remains that—

an accusation until proven otherwise by a competent court," Northwood rubbished the state's narrative.

Minfiled rose to protest.

"State, you have had your time. Objection is sustained. There are a lot of gaps in your submission. In the absence of acceptable written evidence, everything you've submitted remains the subject of hearsay and open to scrutiny. I, therefore, dismiss it as inadmissible as proof of wrongdoing in support of your prayer for the denial of bail for the accused," Her Worship read the facts in a razor-sharp tone. "Do you have anything else to say?" she asked, holding a pen in one hand while the other gesticulated to Minfiled.

"Your Worship, the state is opposed to bail. Considering the gravity of the case, we insist that the accused is a flight risk and may interfere with witnesses," the state submitted.

Magistrate Wayford asked for closing statements from both the state and the defence.

"Your Worship, we are dealing with a possible criminal case here. There are potential immigration issues, and from the face of it, there are many other matters arising, pointing to the fact that the defendant has a case to answer. Therefore, in the spirit of protecting and not exposing the complainant, the accused must be remanded in custody.

"Need we remind you of how disrespectful the accused was in his initial appearance before this court? We pray that you remand him in custody, Your Worship," the state submitted.

"We have no further submissions, Your Worship," Northwood said, enjoying the game, as Minfiled was seething, visibly angry.

Magistrate Wayford called for a thirty-minute adjournment. After exactly 30 minutes, all were seated in the packed courtroom. When the magistrate entered using the door leading to her office, they all rose as per procedure and waited for her to take her seat, then sat down again.

The magistrate didn't take time: "I have carefully listened to submissions from both parties. Strong and passionate positions have been taken by both sides, consistent with the law. In deciding whether or not the accused deserves bail, I have considered the gravity of the matter."

She paused, adjusted her spectacles, then continued:

"Clearly, the matter is grave, and threatens our social order, peace and tranquillity. The United Kingdom prides itself in being a champion of equal rights. Our laws protect not only British citizens but all who live in the UK. The law does not tolerate any breach of human rights,"

She paused again. The defence was in panic mode. Nothing was predictable anymore. The state appeared buoyant, the initial opening remarks seemingly favouring its position. In their view, the positive remarks, the emphasis on law and the protection of all inhabitants of the UK reflected the position that justice would be served and that society must be preserved.

After what appeared to be eternity, Magistrate Wayford continued. "Due to the complexity of this matter, I have decided to take more time to allow a process that will bring a just judgment regarding the bail application. I am, therefore, adjourning this court. Bail verdict will be heard in three weeks' time.

Everyone was stunned. Both the state and the defence had anticipated denial of bail. It was as clear as daytime. Three weeks was a long time, particularly to John. In spite of all his debauchery, he was aware that he had crossed the red line. He desperately wanted to talk to Sharon. But it was too late. The damage had already been done. Besides, interfering with investigations was a crime. All his electronic gadgets and phones were seized by the police, and his Facebook account was suspended.

Meanwhile, his employer sent notice of termination of contract. It was based on the agreement that the contract could be terminated by either party by giving one month notice, without having to give reasons.

Chapter 25

Time flies, really. Thursday marked exactly three weeks after John was caged in remand prison. Day after day, sadness filled his heart. Sometimes he felt the urge to revenge but an inner voice reassured him that it was all for the good.

Overnight, John was an international newsmaker. Global news feeds got wind of his case, prompting journalists to be on his trail. Also, the International Coalition for Against Abuse of Women raised £3 000 for Sharon's cause. The money wasn't directly managed by her, buy by a trust, whose responsibility was to handle and distribute it in accordance with funding the document.

John prepared to hear the verdict of the bail application. He had sobered up now, having cleared his clogged head. Notwithstanding possible restrictions, he intended to bring his parents and some of his classmates to the UK to facilitate dialogue between him and Sharon, and ask for forgiveness.

But it was too late. The seriousness of his case against the state, rendered it impossible to collapse through withdrawal. The only viable route was bribing the state counsel, but this too was a tall order. State lawyers were promoted on the basis of their competency. Besides, the lawyers would have to find a technicality, otherwise any misstep to weaken the case would cause massive complications.

An hour before the set court time, John was served with summons. Sharon had instructed her lawyers to raise more allegations; two criminal ones regarding cyberbullying, and possession of critical information about another person constituting breach of privacy. And a civil one in Zimbabwe in which she was claiming US$1,5 million against him, for tearing a family apart through exposing the gossip that was in her phone to relatives.

She was also suing him for £1,6 million for the psychological trauma she suffered. John had seven days to settle or prepare for a protracted court case. Sharon did not have to worry about the costs for litigation as she had funding coming in.

That afternoon, John went to court to hear his bail ruling. He was in low spirits quieter and lacked any willpower to fight. Sharon's claim was significant and her position factual, though the valuation and quantum was debatable. He clearly knew that the case was easy to prove, probably stalling only at the compensation phase.

Chapter 26

The setup remained the same in Court 8, with Magistrate Wayford sitting in her high back hardwood and exotic leather chair in her usual demeanour. Only that she wasn't wearing black but donned an azure, blue suit and a matching blouse. The occasion was probably different. It was judgment day on a matter so delicate.

Just about the time she settled in to pass judgment on John Dube's bail application, noise erupted just outside the courtroom. Normally judicial officers do not bother themselves about noises outside the court, but in recent years, events tended to transpire outside courts, with serious implications.

Magistrate Wayford did the unthinkable. She stopped the session and declared a recess, a practice not common, though not difficult to imagine. Many reasons can be put forward, such as illness of the accused, illness of the judicial officer, or an emergency, which, in his or her estimation warrants adjournment.

"This court is adjourned; we resume at 3:45pm." Her Worship declared, standing up to leave.

Outside, the International Coalition Against Abuse of Women had besieged the court. They held placards, chanted slogans and sang in declaration that no bail should be given to a molester. The women's protest was being screened live on major news networks across the world.

Magistrate Wayford removed her gown, and went to the street to watch from a safe distance. She was protected by three officers. She wanted to make an informed opinion. That afternoon, she called the Chief Justice for a discussion over the phone, which was unusual. She assessed the impact of releasing John on bail given the reports on TV channels, the state's initial case and the demonstration.

After much contemplation, she returned to her chair and proceedings resumed on time.

Without wasting time, she ruled: "The accused's bail application is hereby granted."

The defence did not immediately express joy as they were waiting for the conditions, which came by-and-by

"You are to surrender your passport. You are strictly prohibited from contacting the complainant directly or indirectly. You are to report to Manchester Metropolitan Police Station once a week and pay a bail fee of £5 000 plus £5 000 for contempt of court. Do you have anything to say?" the magistrate asked.

"The burden is too heavy to carry for your servant, Your Worship. Please consider reducing the bail to £1 000 and waive the contempt of court charges," he pleaded.

After careful consideration, she said, "The bail fee is reduced to £1 500, but the contempt charges and fees stand. These are separate matters. You can negotiate terms for settlement up to the end of day on Friday next week failure of which you will be imprisoned.

Chapter 27

The government of Zimbabwe had been battling reduction in direct foreign investment (FDI). The diaspora community offered a solution through remittances back to the country for various reasons. Some bought land and constructed homes. Others simply sent money back home for upkeep of relatives while others were repaying the debts that had accumulated.

The government managed to formulate policies that were sound to guarantee that funds sent through will be received by the local recipient in United States dollars.

One morning the Governor of the Reserve Bank of Zimbabwe and the Minister of Finance, Economic Development and Investment Promotion had a meeting to discuss possible ways in which direct remittances could be used in part or in full to finance government programmes. The meeting was held at the Ministry of Finance offices at the N Government Complex (Mgandane Dlodlo Building).

All stakeholders were seated at exactly 10am. In attendance were directors of policy and macroeconomic planning at the Reserve Bank of Zimbabwe, while a team from the Ministry of Finance comprised directors of fiscal planning and other officials from the budget office.

Minister Nakube, who was chairing, called the meeting to order and asked Madam Linda Ganda to give the opening prayer.

She prayed so passionately, agonisingly and pleadingly that the spirit of God could be felt in the boardroom. It was almost visible—so palpable that they could feel the Lord's presence among them, or at least that's what prayer accomplishes for the faithful.

When Madam Ganda finished praying, everyone looked sober. It was such a powerful prayer that everyone was moved. It created the impression that all were servants of the Most High, regardless of position or station in life, which was critical for the discussions at hand.

"Thank you so much for such a passionate prayer, ma'am. I did not know that the ministry had such powerful prayerful women," Minister Nakube remarked.

He had toned down from his initial flair when he arrived.

"Ladies and Gentlemen, I acknowledge the presence of the Governor of the Reserve Bank of Zimbabwe, Dr Pepukai Marinda, and his team of experts." The minister said.

" Perhaps, we should get straight into the agenda?" Dr Nakube suggested.

There was a brief silence as the **RBZ** Governor was getting ready, then he started: "Ladies and Gentlemen, we are all aware that the country has suffered a significant reduction in its United States dollar earnings due to a significant reduction in exports as industries are shutting down and those that remained open have scaled down significantly.

"Our exports have become increasingly expensive due to our USD cost structure and inefficient equipment, which has had a huge cost build-up," Dr Marinda explained.

He opened a bottle of water and took to quick swigs before continuing:

"We have observed that diaspora remittances have increased astronomically, starting off at just below US$100 million, shooting past the US$1 billion mark to US$2 billion annually. Recipients have been receiving this money in US dollars. We believe that we are the only ones doing so in the region.

"I propose that since we have made tremendous progress towards mono-currency, hence stabilising our currency, the need for a new policy direction arises. We should, therefore, gather the courage to make it compulsory that the USD is preserved by the Central Bank while the recipients are paid in local currency for all inbound transfers."

He took two more gulps of water and scanned the boardroom for any dissenters.

Although the elephant in the room was huge enough for everyone to see, no one had the guts to call it by its name. It was fatal.

An awkward silence reverberated across the room.

"Governor, do you have the details of the banks involved?" Minister Nakube asked rhetorically to break the ice.

"Well, the plan will most likely face a number of tests. Firstly, there is a significant confidence deficit emanating from the hyperinflationary period up to 2008, when the Central Bank raided Nostro accounts under a compulsory acquisition spree in exchange for worthless bearer cheques. This was followed by the issuing of new bank notes and coins which failed to store any value," a director from the Ministry of Finance remarked.

He had stirred a Hornet's nest, and there was no stopping now. The Hornets were already on a rampage. The only way was forward, for retreating meant weakness and risking massive stinging. Receiving no response, the director continued.

"Under the leadership of Dr JPJ, the Central Bank introduced bond notes and coins meant to facilitate ease of change for US dollar transactions. It then printed the notes, which were presumed to be at par with US dollars and deposited into the same account. Experts called it commingling, warning that bad money would eventually chase good money. Later, the Bank separated the two and distinguished them as the Nostro Local and Nostro International. The Nostro Vostro system was breached in the process. The sad part is that those who had deposited actual US dollars in the commingling account, were considered to have deposited Bond Notes, thus losing hundreds of thousands of their hard-earned money," the director drove his point home.

The Governor sensed the urge to respond: "Look here, comrade, those who made those decisions saw it fit to do so, but we cannot be held back because some wrong decisions were made in the past. We must move on as a nation. We cannot be held back by our past," he charged.

"Well Dr, we are one team here. I am only recreating a vivid picture of what we are up against," the director from the ministry reasoned.

"What are your fears, son?" the Governor switched to a fatherly tone, but the expression on his face was that of urgency.

He wanted answers—solutions— and not references to past missteps.

"Well Dr, we have serious concerns about wide usage of the Zimbabwe Gold (ZiG) currency. I believe we have not been able to circulate it enough and that prices are still being pegged in US dollars. There will be a compelling argument that recipients will still need USD, especially for payment of school fees, purchase of building materials, fuel, and passport applications, among others. The real risk comes mainly from merchants who once operated in internet cafes, and benefitted a lot, when funds cease coming through the formal system. Bank commissions will shrink and official tracking will be a nightmare," the director said.

The Governor looked at him with admiration for his boldness, but made a mental note of his divergent views.

"You have a point man, young man. But we still need to run the country. What should be done? What would be your advice? the Governor asked.?

"My view is that confidence cannot be legislated or enforced. We shouldn't compel but build confidence. Allowing continued use of United States dollars will build confidence in the system, hence anchoring our currency," the director replied.

The following day the story leaked on social media forcing remittances to collapse by fifty percent, owing to panic, although they eventually rose.

In the week that followed, there was a roadshow in the UK with the Zimbabwe Investment Promotion Institute promoting investments back home. The organisers faced fierce resistance. The diaspora community did not trust the financial system in Zimbabwe given t past experiences. They did not take it lightly that they were banished from voting, yet their financial contribution was required to move the country forward.

Chapter 28

As weeks turned into months and months into years, Sharon's world appeared to be taking an upward trajectory, which somehow crumbled, prompting her to leave the United Kingdom in a huff.

In the interim, she had started a construction business with Moline Chimbekeya, her childhood friend. Their business model was simple but profitable. They imported building materials from China, and work with a team of expert builders. Their task was to secure clients in the diaspora where payments would be made to almost anywhere in the world.

Moline had a marriage of convenience with Mark Osumo, a Nigerian man, to facilitate his permanent resident status in Zimbabwe and make it easier for him to operate his business. The two had a lavish traditional wedding, attended by scores of her relatives and friends, and solemnised by Pastor Trevor Jambwa of the Apostolic Church of Believers International, a registered marriage officer, under the Marriages Act [Chapter 5:17]. The videos of the ceremony showing the 'lovebirds' signing their nuptials and raising the marriage certificate went viral on social media platforms.

The idea was, perhaps, not only to consummate their marriage, but to create an impression of conviviality, thus keeping business rivals and authorities at bay.

Three months later, Moline visited Nigeria to meet Mark's parents. She was welcomed like a queen, and a plush ceremony was thrown for her the Nigerian way. As expected in today's world of likes, the videos were splashed on social media platforms. She was living the life, and at the same time leaving a trail of convenience. But matters of the heart are strange—opportuneness turned to love. Isn't it that mothers teach their daughters: you will learn to love him? So, it was with Moline. She fell in love with Mark over time, and even demanded that their union of pretence be turned into a matrimony. Mark seemed to feel the same and he put Moline in the family way. Thus, two years after the wedding, Mark Junior was born.

That was the genesis of their construction business, which Sharon later joined as a thirty-five percent shareholder. The business went well for six months, as it benefitted from their picture-perfect teamwork. But as they say, the human mind is complex; it runs deeper than the ocean.

During the course of their business, as usual, Moline, who usually did the orders, had a huge consignment purchased in China ready for loading. Considering the value involved, she decided to be hands-on. She had to fly to China.

She took a flight to the Asian economic powerhouse aboard Sahara Africa airline, in an economy class. The indirect flight was via Lusaka, Zambia, enroute to Kenya for an hour's stopover, and finally Guangzhou, China.

Moline and her friend Sharon were thrilled; their business was poised for a huge take-off. They aimed for the stars, and the sky wasn't even their limit. For Sharon, it would be goodbye to the British Bottom Cleaners (BBC) brigade.

Upon arrival at Guangzhou International Airport, Moline went through immigration formalities. There appeared to be a security glitch. An airport security team intercepted her and one of them escorted her to an office. Not suspecting anything, she walked casually in and produced her passport as proof of identity as required.

"Ma'am, are you Moline Osumo?" a Chinese port security officer asked firmly.

"Yes," she replied innocently, before asking, "Is there a problem ma'am?"

"We have flagged your bag for potentially containing substances that may be prohibited in the People's Republic of China," the security officer said calmly but intently.

"We are going to search your bags, but before we do so, there are a few background questions we would like to ask you," she continued.

"That's okay, officer. Please take your time, I will answer all the questions you may possibly have," Moline said calmly.

Just about that time, Moline's mobile phone buzzed. It was a WhatsApp call from Mark. She asked to be excused for a moment.

"Hey love, I have landed at Guangzhou International Airport but there is a holdup. The airport security suspect that I might be carrying drugs or something prohibited in China," Moline informed Mark.

"Don't worry babe. These are just routine searches," he reassured her. "Call me when done."

"You should be on standby, honey. I have a hunch that there could be something in the bag. Remember, this is not my first time here. I have visited China on business several times, but I have never been held for whatever reason," Moline said, almost in tears.

"Call me when done, babe. I am getting into a meeting now," Mark insisted.

Moline was now unsettled. She wondered why her husband would be busy and appear unalarmed when she needed him most. It wasn't adding up. She had heard a lot of stories about women who were arrested on account of smuggling drugs but she never paid attention.

She decided to call Sharon.

"Hey Mels", Sharon answered immediately. "Are you there yet?"

"Hi Shels. Yes, I am at the airport. But I have been held up by the immigration security on suspicion of smuggling. They're about to search my bags.

"Eish! That sounds bad. Chinese port security rarely stops travellers for no reason. Their surveillance and scanning technologies are advanced. I trust it's not what I'm thinking," Sharon said, alarmed, and I hope Mark isn't involved too.

Having given her enough time on the phone, the security went about their business.

"They're searching now, and it seems there is nothing to worry about," Moline informed Sharon who was still online. "Maybe I was just being-."

"Ma'am, may you please come over here?" the first security officer said, politely, cutting her mid-sentence.

"Are you the one who packed the bags, ma'am?" another officer, a senior one, asked.

"No, ma'am! It was my husband," she replied. "Could there be a problem?"

There was a problem, all right. It was there for everyone to see—a stash of whitish powder stuffed in a false compartment underneath the base of her travelling bag. Preliminary investigations of the substances in three separate packets were pointing to cocaine and heroin. Moline sweated.

"Ma'am, here we are. The substances found in one of your bags are believed to be prohibited drugs in this country, carrying a heavy penalty if confirmed," she said. "I'm afraid, ma'am," she continued, almost regrettably, "you are under detention. You will be detained here until our narcotics team arrive. Meanwhile, you may inform your relatives of the development."

Sharon, who heard everything, was shocked. She tried calling Mark but his number went unanswered. She called two of Mark's friends and none of them could confirm his whereabouts. It was becoming apparent that he had set Moline up.

Thirty minutes later, the narcotics team arrived for further questioning and tests, which came out positive for cocaine and heroin. Thus, Moline was arrested, pending court appearance in a foreign land intolerant of hard drugs, possession or dealing of which carried the death penalty. Her world collapsed, shattering her dreams.

Meanwhile, someone had to rescue the consignment, for life doesn't end with an individual's departure. The world moves on, unperturbed. The task fell on Sharon's shoulders as one of the three shareholders of the company.

She had to take the first flight available to China from Heathrow Airport. The situation had to be saved, particularly the cargo.

Chapter 29

It was a busy week for Ambassador Tichaona Nyamapanga, a decorated career diplomat, who had dedicated his life for the nation.

An easy-going, short and razor-sharp man with an elephant's memory, his life revolved around the protection of Zimbabwe. He was known to navigate complex diplomatic standoffs involving the motherland. He was once posted to the United Kingdom at a time relations between Harare and London were at their lowest.

Amb Nyamapanga established somewhat cordial relations between the two nations, even when Zimbabwe embarked on the post-2000 Fast Track Land Reform Programme, aimed at correcting historical imbalances in land ownership. Indigenous black people, who were in the majority, were displaced from their fertile arable ancestral land and relocated to arid tsetse-fly infested regions, while the minority white settlers claimed rich soils for themselves and their descendants—a status quo they wanted to maintain at all cost.

Land has always been a thorny issue in Zimbabwe, formerly Rhodesia, stretching back to 1890 when the country was colonised by Britain. It was the major reason for the First Chimurenga of the 1890s and the Second Chimurenga of the 1970s. It was only a matter of time, therefore, that the willing-seller willing-buyer policy soon after independence in 1980 and other earlier reforms on land, would be overtaken by events.

The true owners of the land were becoming impatient that what they fought for in the protracted liberation struggle was taking too long to be realised, thus they decided to reclaim it by force. Stunning the world, they set maize and wheat fields on fire in their march towards total freedom through landownership. And, as expected, the backlash from Western capitals was instant. Aware of the hunger for land and its justification, the Government later regularised the process.

For close to 20 years, there were struggles on the farms. Most beneficiaries sold all the livestock and equipment they found there, leaving the farmland in a sorry state. Despite government support through inputs, the farms were so run down that the image created pleased the dispossessed white former commercial farmers as it fell into their narrative— blacks were not farmers. In fact, it was interpreted through the imperialistic view that blacks were incapable of self-rule, and would turn the farms into wasteland and make the country a shithole in no time if given an opportunity.

The sentiments seemed to resonate with Ian Douglas Smith's illusion that there will never be majority rule in Rhodesia (Zimbabwe) in his lifetime; that of his children and grandchildren. "Never in a thousand years," he declared. But in just 14 years, he was forced to eat humble pie. If it so happened that the country fell into the hands of black people, he is said to have argued, roads would become impassable; there would be so much poverty that people would die of hunger, as production on farmland plummet. Sewage, he added, would flow everywhere, even into people's homes.

Months after the first wave of land appropriation, the country's economy tanked, as the West retaliated through punitive illegal economic sanctions. The United States of America passed the Zimbabwe Democracy and Economic Recovery Act (ZIDERA) in 2001, which blocked Zimbabwe from getting loans, credit or any financial help from the World Bank, International Monetary Fund, or any major global financial institution. The European Union followed suit, thus bringing the motherland to its knees. Ordinary citizens suffered as the weight of sanctions bit in.

However, the story started changing for the better. Realising that relying on rainfed agriculture was soon becoming problematic due to climate change, the new government of President Kufazvinei resorted to irrigation through its own initiatives and public-private partnerships (PPPs). In no time, vast tracks of land were put under irrigation, greening the countryside and farmlands once again. Annual tobacco production surged to 100 million kilogrammes, then 315 million kilogrammes, all powered by blacks, the real owners of the land.

Road construction and rehabilitation work commenced and One-Stop-Border-Posts were constructed. The Beitbridge Border Post was modernised and the Beitbridge-Harare Highway was rehabilitated. On the aviation sector, the Joshua Mqabuko Nkomo International Airport, Victoria Falls International Airport, and the Robert Gabriel Mugabe International Airport were revamped; while domestic airline routes re-established.

President Kufazvinei beamed with pride when he commissioned the refurbished Robert Gabriel Mugabe International Airport: "Airport *yedu inomwisa mvura. Anongori manyezu nyakata nguvo dzemwenga akasvika zuro, kudakadza mweso.*"

Tourist arrivals doubled in less than five years, a clear indication of black people's ability to achieve when left alone to decide and define their destiny through hard work, unity and patriotism. Indeed, colonialists cannot define blacks' capability through white lenses.

Investments in power generation increased production at Hwange Thermal Power Station, which saw Unit 7 and Unit 8 being expanded at a cost of over US$1 billion.

In agriculture, wheat production rose astronomically to a record-breaking 639 000 tonnes in the 2025 season, making Zimbabwean self-sufficient, and ultimately, a net exporter.

* * *

Amb. Nyamapanga was reflecting on all the struggles and victories the nation had gone through. He diligently and patriotically served as Zimbabwe's envoy to the United States of America, Sweden, Australia, South Africa, China and Japan. His train of thoughts was interrupted by his personal assistant, informing him that there was a direct call for him coming in.

Immediately, his desk phone rang. He picked it at the second ring with a shaky hand. The Chinese Ambassador to Zimbabwe Mr Wang Xi, whom he closely interacted with during his tenure in China, wanted to discuss something urgently with him at the Chinese Embassy in Mount Pleasant, Harare. The matter involved Zimbabweans arrested in China for smuggling drugs, among other serious offences. Trouble! the Ambassador thought as he left his office. He asked his PA to call his driver at once.

The ambassador left his Munhumutapa Building offices and sat in the front passenger seat of his official Land Cruiser vehicle. He was accompanied by the chief director for protocol and the director for communication and advocacy in the Ministry of Foreign Affairs and International Trade. The guzzler headed straight to the Embassy of the People's Republic of China along Golden Stairs Road. Upon arrival, he was welcomed at the entrance by Mr Wang Xi.

A seasoned diplomat, Amb. Nyamapanga was at the forefront of local efforts to complement the sterling job being done by Ambassador Tobias Ngwenya, who was the Zimbabwean envoy to the People's Republic of China then.

The meeting was attended by two more people from the Chinese Embassy, making it three from each part The atmosphere was tense. Zimbabwe and China had been all-weather friends since the time of the liberation struggle against Ian Smith's oppressive regime, with China playing the role of a big brother, offering training, tactical and logistical support to the cause. China assisted Zimbabwe in a number of other key governance and economic areas after independence in 1980.

"We're here to discuss a matter too heavy to contemplate seeing how deep how relations are.

China and Zimbabwe share a long, great friendship premised on mutual cooperation, development, uplifting of our peoples and promotion of grassroot development," Amb. Xi began.

"The Chinese people take the China-Zimbabwe relationship seriously, as evidenced by our investments in education, mining, agriculture, cultural exchanges and technology transfer programmes. This shows how committed China is to the uplifting of the Zimbabwean people, who reciprocate it all in many commendable ways.

"China heartly congratulates the people of Zimbabwe on the occasion of their 46th Independence Day anniversary celebrated recently. As a people, we are aware of what it took for your nation to get where you are today."

The ambassador paused and straightened up, allowing his introductory words to take effect. A diplomat par excellence, he remained steady and respectful, despite the gravity of the matter at hand.

"Thank you ambassador for your remarks," Amb. Nyamapanga said. The Government of Zimbabwe thanks the People's Republic of China for the tremendous friendship that has subsisted between our great nations for many years. The people of Zimbabwe honour the people of China and hold them dearly, deeply, respectfully and admirably. Our friendship, profoundly rooted in seeking what is best for our peoples, is based on trust, mutual respect and cooperation in which collective prosperity is the ultimate goal.

"The people of Zimbabwe value all that, and, we believe nothing can come between us. We have such an unshakeable bond and our commitment to that friendship is cast in iron."

"Thank you ambassador for your feedback and reactions. "We, indeed, share a special relationship, yet here we are, facing an inextricable deadlock," said Amb Xi thoughtfully.

There are more than two hundred Zimbabweans jailed in China. Most, if not all, having committed a crime whose penalty is death. The people of China find themselves in a hard place because of that.

"If it were up to me, as many Chinese would have wished, I would free them. But we are a law-abiding nation—we respect the rule of law as constitutionally defined without fear or favour," Amb Xi said in a measured tone.

He was fighting the urge to shed tears, yet despite that, a tear dropped from his left eye and lingered on his cheek, while another from his right eye had already bolted and landed on his pair of trousers and disappeared like a raindrop in a desert.

The ambassador's tears appeared to be a premonition of a bad omen he had no power over. It was symbolic of both helplessness in the face of disaster and a willingness to help the people of Zimbabwe, even in their darkest hour. Yet, he was bound by the law; by the Constitution of the People's Republic of China. Zimbabweans were most welcome in China, but laws of hospitality have their own limitations. When it comes to the protection of his own family, their identity and sovereignty, the host may be called upon to stab or shoot his guest if certain red lines are crossed. That was the situation Amb. Xi found himself in.

"The people of Zimbabwe fully respect the laws and regulations of your great nation, without which there could not have been any China to talk about. The law and order in your country has made it what it is today," Amb. Nyamapanga said. Yet, in the same stroke, even friends look at each other with favour.

"Moments like these, shape the relationship; based on mercy, forbearing, longsuffering, and a demonstration that, though we may wrong each other, we seek clemency, pardon, and camaraderie. Stronger bonds are fashioned in trying times where uncertainty lingers on.

"I have come here bearing a white banner of peace; a banner of rapprochement and entente to the people of your great nation.

I humbly submit the plea of the people of Zimbabwe: May you please spare the lives of our fellow citizens and deport them, so that they can be dealt with in accordance with the laws of Zimbabwe?"

There was silence in the room. The Ambassador of the People's Republic of China to Zimbabwe was conflicted in his heart. He saw the pain and agonising begging of Amba Nyamapanga, and understood him well. He had been in the country for three years and was aware of how Zimbabweans respected the sanctity of life. He had enjoyed many freedoms; the heartfelt welcome and the warmth of the people of Zimbabwe. The more he thought of it, the more he felt a heavy load on his shoulders. He wanted to show that he cared; he wanted to return the favour, and above all, he wanted to reciprocate what had been done for him and his family. But he was aware that in a country of more than 1,4 billion people, two hundred foreign nationals were like tiny flies, which can be killed in one swift swish of the hand and instantly forgotten. Besides, he was aware of how the law worked.

The ambassador shifted his gaze and silently clasped his hands. His limitations were right before him. He was helpless.

"Ambassador, there could be a way of working around it, subject to approval at the highest level of authority, of course. There are Chinese people serving sentences for drug offences here, who can be freed on a person-to-person basis with Zimbabweans jailed in China for similar cases of wrongdoing," Amb Nyamapanga said.

There was something in his eyes. It was neither fear nor pity. He knew the weight of the burden he was carrying—two hundred people with the hangman's noose around their necks—his fellow countrymen. Their images, exchanged in the course of the meeting on a huge screen in the boardroom at the Chinese Embassy, with the youngest of them only 19 years old, haunted him. He felt for their families and loved ones. Yet, like Amb Xi, he was also aware of his limitations.

Sometime during the tenure of Gordon Brown as the United Kingdom premier, it was reported that a British citizen was found in possession of drugs in China, tried and swiftly sentenced to death. It is said that Brown tried to intervene at head of state and government level with his Chinese counterpart to no avail. The law had to be followed to the letter without fear or favour, he was informed. And in the end, the errant British national was executed.

Amb. Nyamapanga was well aware of it. He knew he was performing a Japanese kabuki dance.

"Ambassador, I am deeply grateful for the honour of working in your country, and the respect you have bestowed upon me personally is of great value to my family," Amb. Xi said. "Had it been in my power, I would have freed your people. However, the best I can do is to appeal for postponement of execution, hoping that conditions may change with the passage of time in terms of the law and policy.

"I will submit your proposal for exchange of prisoners to the Foreign Minister. But to be frank with you, China does not tolerate nationals who commit crimes in other countries. There is a higher chance that they will receive a harsher punishment on arrival."

There were no immediate reactions from Ambassador Nyamapanga and his team. They were all aware of Chinese laws and the position on exchange of prisoners. Anyway, there was no harm in trying.

When Amb. Nyamapanga finally spoke, his voice was not low—neither loud nor inaudible. He was speaking from the heart.

"Ambassador, we have a rich history of mutual cooperation since the liberation struggle. The bond of friendship created has been the glue that held us together. Our great nation is endowed with vast minerals, which your country needs for economic growth and prosperity; gold, platinum, lithium, palladium, steel, among many others to agricultural products.

"You have in us, a friend, who understands your needs and has been putting your nation ahead of others. This friendship, while it should not be abused, forms the basis of how we deal with each other. Just as we have put your country ahead of others, we too believe wholeheartedly that for a friend like you, we have a chance to talk in a more favourable manner than anyone else," Amb. Nyamapanga remarked.

He looked the Chinese Ambassador in the eye for several moments, as if in a staring contest. Delegates from both sides were aware of the intimidatory trick.

"Ambassador, we are appreciative of the relationships and the many business opportunities we have secured as the people of China in your great country. But to weaponise the relationship and demand feather beddings is to play it unfair.

"We have invested in your country through agriculture mechanisation programmes. We have constructed and refurbished your major airports and assisted in military infrastructure at a time international lenders were shunning your country.

"We have been a loyal friend and comrade in tough times. I believe, therefore, that we should find a non-threatening solution to transform our great countries for the greater good," Amb Xi said.

There was a moment of silence. Amb. Nyamapanga had learnt that speaking too soon pre-empted a man's strongpoint. He wanted his counterpart to absorb the silence and create awkwardness, that when he finally spoke, his words were well-received and eagerly awaited. It was a tactic similar to the ceremonial weigh-in in boxing, without the face-off, of course.

"Ambassador, we require a definitive position. We consider life sanctimonious in our country, and expect our friends to understand that. We propose the exchange of prisoners, and beseech you to make a decree that specifically differentiates Zimbabwe as a key ally, enjoying special treatment,"Amb. Nyamapanga said with finality to resounding silence.

"Ambassador, China has committed millions of dollars towards the mechanisation of agriculture and mining in Zimbabwe, in addition to investments in power generation worth more than US$1 billion. The People's Republic of China has also provided a US$140 million grant through China-Aid for the construction of the New Parliament Building in Mount Hampden, among other infrastructure developments, which make your request not only preposterous, but deeply regrettable," Amb. Xi said knowledgeably.

"We are on the same page, ambassador, as friends are wont to. The people of Zimbabwe are grateful for what the People's Republic of China has done for our country through mutual cooperation and investments in agriculture, mining, power generation and other key infrastructural projects. Zimbabwe has also reciprocated through concessions that have made our cooperation mutual. China is our country's largest importer of lithium," Amb. Nyamaropa said calmly, changing tact.

"We acknowledge, Your Excellence, that Chinese conglomerates have invested over US$1, 1 billion into Zimbabwe's lithium sector, fronting local value-addition initiatives like Prospect Lithium Zimbabwe's US$400 million processing plant at Arcadia Lithium Mine in Goromonzi, Mashonaland East Province."

He paused to gauge the impact of his words. Satisfied, he continued:

"As we speak, and as you are also aware of, Prospect Lithium Zimbabwe, which is owned by Zhejiang Huayou Cobalt, has started exporting its first lithium sulphate batch, marking the country's inaugural production of lithium salt, boosting our push towards local beneficiation, following our ban on raw lithium exports.

"Our citizens are also benefitting from the opening up of markets for their agricultural produce in China as well as other opportunities in business, technology and education; the reason why they frequent your great country.

"For those reasons, ambassador, I find it, eh, for lack of a better word, illogical, that we should cut such fruitful ties owing to two hundred errant citizens. It is within your power to save them, ambassador; for the sake of our strong ties, for the sake of the future, for the sake of our peoples. What would happen should Zimbabwe retaliate drastically to your killing of its citizens?"

Am Nyamapanga paused, took a sip from the glass of water in front of him, and scanned the room. There was something about the way he asked—he was either stating a fact or testing the waters.

Reading the room, Amb. Xi smiled, clasped, then unclasped his hands, and finally said: "Ambassador, your request has been noted. You will hear from us in the next three weeks. Since there are no more contributions coming, I declare this meeting closed," he said.

According to The Africa Report dated 19 May, 2016, the Parliamentary Portfolio Committee on Women Affairs, Gender and Community Development confirmed that Zimbabwean women in Chinese prisons were mainly married to Nigerian nationals who allegedly used them for drug trafficking.

It is believed that some were willing participants, while others are unconsciously used as mules by their husbands, who secretly pack drugs in their luggage before departure to purported shopping trips in China, which would be switched upon safe arrival. Unfortunately, well-equipped and competent Chinese immigration officials easily detect the drugs. They are said to have profiled nations based on the number of cases intercepted. That red list allows them to be thorough at the port of entry.

The number of Zimbabwean women arrested for drug trafficking is unknown, although the Ministry of Foreign Affairs and International Trade insisted that less than ten Zimbabweans, mostly women were arrested in China for drug trafficking. While figures varied owing largely to late updates or identity theft, scores of Zimbabwean nationals were arrested for drug trafficking and were facing the death penalty.

Speaking at a press conference, Parliamentary Portfolio Committee on Women Affairs, Gender and Community Development chairperson, Honourable Beverly Nyamapanga, confirmed that China was holding one thousand stranded Zimbabwean women for drug trafficking offences.

She confirmed that two hundred Zimbabweans, mainly women, were on death row in China, for drug trafficking. Their fate had been blamed on marriages of convenience with Nigerian men, who promised them flashy lifestyles.

Lately, debate has been raging in Zimbabwe on whether unions between local women and Nigerian men should be prohibited, or stiffer regulations be applied to curb the abuse of the Marriages Act. However, regulating love matters has never been known to work anywhere in the world.

The Africa Report maintained that China was not the only country where Zimbabwean women were stranded. Recent reports showed that Zimbabwean woman were equally stranded in countries like Kuwait, after they were promised lucrative jobs. There were over 2 000 of them roaming around China and other countries, where they would have gone willingly or trafficked.

China is renowned to be ruthless on drug traffickers. According to Amnesty International, the Asian country tops globally when it comes to execution of offenders. About two hundred Zimbabwean women were recently rescued from human trafficking rings in Kuwait, where they were lured on false promises of employment, and some have already been repatriated back home. Some were initiated into prostitution while others were use as housemaids.

In some situations, the housemaid would be used as a sex object by any member of the family for free.

Cases in which Zimbabweans were arrested for drug trafficking in countries like China, India and Cyprus, among others, were so rampant that they dominated proceedings in the National Assembly for many years. In one such case, a Zimbabwean woman was caught with two kilogrammes of cocaine worth US$1,5 million at Delhi Airport in India.

The Ministry of Foreign Affairs and International Trade also grappled with the issue.

The permanent secretary in the ministry, Mr Norman Tavonga, expressed dismay at the number of Zimbabwean nationals arrested for drug trafficking in countries like China and India.

"We have received reports that ten Zimbabweans were arrested in China for drug trafficking, with at least three women on death row in Beijing," he told journalists.

He also made reference to South Africa, where three Zimbabweans were

arrested for smuggling R2 million worth of heroin into the country through Beitbridge Border Post. The cases were too numerous to mention, particularly involving women, creating a diplomatic disaster for the ministry, Mr Tavonga added.

Drugs usually trafficked included cocaine, heroin, crystal methamphetamine and amphetamine.

On August 5, 2024, NewsDay, a local newspaper, reported that a 31-year-old Zimbabwean man was facing life imprisonment in Australia for smuggling nearly nine hundred kilogrammes of methamphetamine worth a staggering US$828 million, concealed in industrial machines imported from the United States.

"At least 16 Zimbabwean women are stuck in jails across Asian countries, with 14 of them convicted of drug trafficking, which carries the death penalty, while two others have their cases under trial," the permanent secretary concluded.

Chapter 30

John's case was moved from the magistrates' Court to the Crown Court following an application by the state on the basis of jurisdiction, considering the seriousness of the crime; warranting a maximum sentence of ten years on conviction.

The UK system provides that in terms of Criminal Charges (Section 2A/4A PHA 1997), all cases start in the Magistrates' Court, but serious cases (4A) can be moved to the Crown Court. The Crown Court has jurisdiction over more serious Section 4A (Stalking involving fear of violence or serious alarm/distress) offences. These are "either-way" offences that can be tried in either the Magistrates' or Crown Court, depending on the severity, with a maximum penalty of 10 years' imprisonment. John Dube's case fell, or at least according to the state, on the Crown Court due to its severity.

The Crown Court in England and Wales handles serious criminal cases, usually following a magistrates' court committal, with a judge and twelve-member jury. The order of proceedings includes the indictment reading (arraignment), prosecution/defence cases, jury verdict, and sentencing. It also hears appeals against conviction/sentence from lower courts.

On the first day of trial, Sharon was preoccupied by her friend Moline's arrest in China, knowing how the rule of law was applied in that country. The presiding judge was His Honour Lord Marshall Lewis a British Australian with Franco Saxon origin dating back to 1155. He was known for his appetite and desire for justice, which earned him respect from both the state and offenders. When offenders are brought before him, they would be guaranteed of a fair trial.

A 12-member jury was selected according to the UK legal custom. In the Crown Court of England and Wales, a jury consists of twelve members of the public selected randomly from the electoral register. Their fundamental role is to act as the "triers of fact," determining whether the defendant is guilty or not guilty of a serious criminal offence based solely on the evidence presented in court.

The jurors listen to evidence, witness testimonies, and expert reports to determine what actually happened.

They deliver a verdict following instructions from the judge on the relevant law. The jury then decides if the defendant is guilty or not guilty. In the discharge of their duty, they are required to remain impartial. Jurors must base their decisions solely on the evidence presented in the courtroom, ignoring any outside information, news reports, or personal biases.

The jury selects a foreperson to manage discussions, act as the spokesperson, and deliver the verdict in open court. They are also expected to reach a decision. While a unanimous verdict (12-0) is preferred, the judge may accept a majority verdict (10-2 or 11-1) if the jury cannot agree after a reasonable period of deliberation.

In the case of John Dube, the twelve members of the jury consisted of seven men and five women. These were selected via the UK's random selection criteria focusing on those that are eligible to be voted.

These were Lilian West, a banker, Vivian Clara Wade, a cruise ship manager, Thomas J Middleton, a headteacher, Bob Carrington Junior, a sports manager at a local school, Norman West, an art collector, Gareth Simpson, Jacob Richardson, Richard Griffith, Susan Hammond, Racheal Hood, an engineer and Jane Towers, a retired barrister turned fast food businessperson.

The twelve selected Jane Towers as their foreperson. She was to lead the discussions and deliberations as per their terms of reference. These were the people that John had to convince that he committed no crime. His life was in their hands; his fate was in their hands.

The members were all waiting purposefully, having all been formally cleared of any criminal offences. They were ready to serve.

"John Dube, you are being charged with stalking, harassment and defamation of Ms Sharon Tapfuma's character. How do you plead?" His Honour Lord Lewis asked.

"I plead not guilty my Lord," he responded.

It was time for opening statements from the accused and the defendant. First, it was the state, represented by Paul Hachingson.

"Your Honour, members of the jury, we have a woman from a country that is close to our hearts; a former colony of our great nation that plunged into economic and social challenges. This young lady here, was brave enough to leave her country in search of a better life here.

"She was certain that she would find work, earn a stable income, and live a peaceful life in the UK. Unfortunately, she was haunted by a man whose high school fantasies have remained stuck in his mind; a man with criminal record; a man who was once arrested for possession of drugs, and was a suspect in underage sexual assault," Hachingson submitted.

"The man has physically assaulted his wife several times and threatened to kill her day in and day out. Witnesses will testify that this man deserves to be taken away from our society into correctional custody after which he deserves to be deported and never again be allowed into our great country."

His words struck differently. They were like a torrent of heavy punches in the gut.

Gerald Macdonald, for the defence, stood up and cleared phlegm from his throat. He was a barrister of great repute, having successfully argued high-profile cases. "Your Honour, members of the Jury," he began.

"The United Kingdom justice system, particularly in England and Wales, is founded on a 1 000-year evolution of legal traditions, primarily featuring a common law system that emphasises independence, impartiality, and the rule of law. The same law recognises the supreme authority of our law premised on the unshakable rock solid founding principle that everyone, including the government and the monarchy, is subject to.

"The same statutes provide that there should be equality before the law. All individuals are treated equally under the law, and courts apply the same legal principles to all citizens. It further establishes and hold true that each member of society is entitled to a fair trial, with evidence presented in open court. The burden of proof in criminal cases lies with the prosecution (the Crown) to prove guilt beyond reasonable doubt."

Macdonald paused, took a depth breathe and turned his eyes towards the judge, not in a disrespectful way, but in acknowledgement of his impartiality. He moved to the jury's section, and, careful not to get too close, he said in a low, almost inaudible but impactful voice:

"Members of the jury, your duty at law is to search for the truth. And the truth is that the accused, a Zimbabwean man, who arrived in the UK 15 years ago, extended his generosity to the complainant whom he had known since primary school. They grew up in the same neighbourhood, sharing a lot in common; just like siblings.

"Having come here earlier than the complainant, the accused sought to assist her, not only as a fellow citizen or child of the soil; mwana wevhu, as they affectionately say back home, but a longtime friend and his mother's child—his sister. That is how he has been raised through the philosophy of Ubuntu/Hunhu, believing that sharing is love and unity is strength. Unfortunately, it was that which got him arrested and arraigned before this court."

Silence echoed across the courtroom. Three or four members of the jury wiped their brows.

The investigating officer, Chief Superintendent Macmillan Griffiths, was the first to testify.

"State your name for the record," the clerk of court said.

"I am Macmillan Griffiths, a Chief Superintendent in the police service, the investigating officer for the State vs Sharon case," he replied.

Hachingson looked at him for a few seconds, turned to the judge, members of the jury, then back at Chief Supt Griffiths. .

"Please tell the court how long you have been in service?" Hachingson asked.

"More than 15 years," He replied immediately.

"Is this your first time to investigate this case, sir?" Hachingson asked.

"I have handled quiet a number of similar cases, approximately ten, three of which being serious criminal ones with a hundred percent conviction rate," the investigating officer replied.

"Objection my Lord. There is no relevance in the long answer," the defence counsel protested.

"Sustained," Lord Lewis ruled. "Chief Superintendent Macmillan Griffiths, please answer the questions as asked."

John was watching the proceedings not knowing what to say or make of the opening submissions from both sides.

"Chief Supt Macmillan Griffiths, tell the court your findings of the case before us," Hachingson said.

"I have submitted our findings and the evidence we have as exhibits to the court. And, I must say, some of the evidence cannot be publicly disclosed since they are nude pictures of the complainant," the IO said.

Sharon shifted in her chair. Although she had seen the pictures, she didn't know how John got them. It puzzled her, yet she found herself agreeing with Hutchinson's line of questioning.

"First, I want to present the call log from where it all started," the investigating officer said.

He handed over a five-page document with calls John made to Sharon. The call log was extracted from his phone and it matched with the records from Sharon's line.

"Chief Supt Macmillan Griffiths, may you please explain what this is all about?" the prosecutor asked.

"The first two and a half pages show calls from John and the second confirm the same as received. The stamp there is from the mobile network service provider, and the attached document is the court order from the Magistrates' Court allowing us to collect the information," Chief Supt Griffiths replied with ease.

"Why do you think this information is necessary to this case?" Hachingson asked.

"Well, the criminal charges are to do with stalking and harassment, the definition of which requires that there should be constant unwanted communication. The calls show, on average, fifteen to thirty missed calls per day during working hours," the IO replied.

"Chief Supt Griffiths, I put it to you, the call log doesn't indicate the fact that the calls were unwanted. Where did you get that notion?" Hachingson asked.

"I took statements from the complainant and she mentioned that she did not want the constant communication," the IO replied.

The investigating officer moved to other exhibits, showing Sharon's nude photos.

"Chief Supt Griffiths can you explain to the court how you got the photographs, and why you believe they are appropriate for this case?" the state lawyer asked determinedly.

"We found the photos in the accused's phone. Sharon gave a statement to the effect that she never sent any photos to him. The accused didn't say where he got them. But he seemed to have had access to the complainant's apartment," the IO said firmly.

"So, what further work did you do to establish what happened?" Hachingson asked.

"We are holding it as part of evidence of the collection of information, and possibly, breach of privacy and holding of sensitive personal data without written consent. Our view is that this may also constitute illegal possession or potential distribution of pornographic material.

"Next, we have Facebook messages retrieved from the accused's account; recordings of sensitive social media conversations between the complainant and her relatives, which the accused hacked into, acquired and distributed," Chief Supt Griffiths said.

Tears welled in Sharon's eyes as the issue of family relations was discussed.

"We also recorded statements from the accused's wife, who said her husband and beaten her up more than three times in a month for the greater part of the time they were in England. She stated that the suspect has videos, cameras, and a lot of other equipment he claims to plant at people's houses to extort them. The police recovered the equipment and he confirmed using it for various purposes, including recording his enemies without elaborating," the investigating officer said.

Hachingson was about to ask another question when the judge interrupted him and adjourned the court.

During the break Sharon checked on Moline. She hoped to talk to her over the phone, but she couldn't. Her trial was scheduled for the following day. She could have travelled to China to offer her morale support, but she had her own demons to face in the UK.

Prisoners in China generally have legal rights to communicate with family via mail and, in some cases, limited, monitored telephone calls, typically after being sentenced and transferred to prison. While regulations allow for communication, access is subject to approval, and privileges like phone calls can be restricted as a form of discipline.

In China, while convicted prisoners may receive calls, those in detention centres (pre-trial) generally cannot make calls to family, though they can meet with lawyers or consular officials.

Moline was in such a situation. She was alone in a foreign land and about to be tried for possession of hard drugs. The court trial was a mere formality. There was sufficient evidence to prove her case beyond reasonable doubt and convict her. She was clearly going to be sentenced to death. There were no two ways about it.

Most Chinese facilities restrict the use of phones. Phone calls are often limited to specific, infrequent intervals and are subject to monitoring. Additional calls beyond authorised limits require special approval.

For foreign inmates in some facilities, for example, Shanghai, calls may be limited to fifteen minutes, with costs covered by the inmate.

In China, point-based systems are often used, where phone privileges can be reduced or cut as punishment. In practice, access to communication is highly controlled and can vary depending on the facility and the nature of the crime.

When the court session resumed, it was the defence's time to cross examine the investigating officer.

"Chief Supt Griffiths, , do you know a gentlemen named Tony MacPherson?" Macdonald asked.

The question caught him off guard.

"Suppose I do, what does that got to do with this case? the IO asked, a little annoyed.

"Anyway, let me refresh your memory. He was your teacher in high school. You disputed his decision to exclude you from a cricket match and you hit him with a baseball stick. In a fit of rage, you went on to hit his dog, killing it instantly," Macdonald narrated.

"That was a long time ago. What has that to do with anything? Your boy will be gone for a long-time, big man. Spare the court your time-wasting tactics", Chief Supt Griffiths said, visibly miffed.

"I put it to you that on 5 December 2000, you were caught in a compromising position with a female co-employee. How do you respond?" MacDonald hit again.

"I am not a saint but I know my work. And, Macdonald, if you're spoiling for a character assassination, I'm in. It's not like everyone here is unaware of your disciplinary case by the Law Society involving misuse of trust funds in your custody. Tell the court who the investigating officer was if you're such a man of integrity," Chief Supt hit back.

"Chief Supt Griffiths, have you been to Africa? Do you know how Africans live?" Macdonald asked casually, dropping his earlier high-pitched, self-importance and all-knowing attitude.

"I have never been there. Was I supposed to go there? Anyway, what's there?" the IO asked.

"The people there live under a concept of Ubuntu/Hunhu in which an individual is defined by his or her humanity towards others. They look out for each other, and when there is a funeral, people from three to four blocks, or villages away will come and hold a vigil until burial. Also, a child is watched over by a society to whom he or she belongs. This is the spirit which inspired the accused and got him in trouble with the law. It was out of love not lust or the desire to destroy," Macdonald submitted.

"Very well, sir! But do they also send damaging information to family social media groups to cause disunity if they live by the so-called Ubuntu? Do they collect nude pictures of each other?" the investigating officer asked.

"You said you found nude photos in the accused's phone; did it occur to you that the complainant could have freely sent them to him as a way of advertising herself to supplement her income?" Macdonald asked.

"Objection", Hachingson protested.

"Sustained," Lord Lewis ruled. "Defence counsel, please stay on course."

"Understood, my Lord," Macdonald said apologetically.

Did it occur to you, sir, that if the complainant. is, indeed, involved in any production and distribution of pornographic material the accused will be an accessory to crime?" Chief Supt Griffiths asked.

Macdonald remained silent.

On the second day of trial, John's wife testified to the beatings, and numerous cases of forced sexual intercourse. She provided video and audio evidence of the death threats that the accused used to make.

She was so eloquent that she brought the jury to tears.

Due to its complexity, the trial dragged on, but one thing was certain: the accused's fate had been sealed—unless new evidence miraculously emerged.

By day six, all the witnesses had testified except Sharon. When she stood up to testify, John stood up and knelt before her asking for forgiveness. He asked to testify ahead of her and his prayer was granted.

"I would like to apologise to Sharon for the destruction of family relationships, the emotional trauma that I caused her, and the time I have wasted for her. She is such a nice person that I still love her from the bottom of my heart. I am sorry for my actions. From the bottom of my heart, I ask for forgiveness and I am willing to sufficiently compensate the complainant should she consider withdrawing the case," John pleaded, much to the defence counsel's horror.

The judge looked at him in astonishment.

"Why now, why plead guilty now?" he asked?

"I am sorry my Lord for wasting the court's time. Consider my change of heart in your judgment. I do not wish to waste much of your time anymore, and the state's resources. I know your duty calls for more deserving cases," John prayed.

When John sat down, the state moved to give its closing submissions.

Hachingson slowly paced to the jury's bench, held fast to the table and said:

"Gentlemen and ladies of the jury, allow me to extend my appreciation of your commitment to national duty. Your resilience, dependability and impartiality in the search for truth have been impressive. The trial that has brought us here today hasn't been any exception in the way the law functions. It has only heightened your mettle. You gathered evidence on what it means to be a woman, a daughter, a sister, and a friend, trying to be a law-abiding breadwinner in a foreign land.

"You know what it means to be stalked, harassed, humiliated and torn from family, all for the sake of a childhood past that refuses to mature. Overwhelming evidence has been led before you. It is your responsibility, once again, to uphold the law and create precedence for our legal system and society," he said before turning to the bench.

"To you, Your Honour and paragon of justice, Lord Lewis, I thank you for your impartiality, patience and wisdom in the upholding of fairness and justice. Once again, the state commits the fate of the law in your capable hands," he said, bowing.

"The state seeks the maximum penalty permissible for such offences. We base our prayer on State vs Matthew Hardy(2022–2026), arguably the largest UK online stalking case. Initially sentenced to nine years in jail, and later reduced to eight in 2022, Hardy caused "psychological terror" to hundreds of victims using fake social media profiles. His case was the subject of the 2024 Netflix documentary *Can I Tell You A Secret?*

"My Lord, allow me, also, to make reference to State vs Karl Chads (October 2024) in which the accused was sentenced to eight years and three months in prison with an extended licence after being deemed "dangerous". Chards stalked a woman he hardly knew and caused her harm through burglary and trespassing.

"In yet another similar case, Oscar Romero (February 2025) was sentenced to 20 weeks' imprisonment at Kingston Upon Thames Crown Court, followed by a 10-year restraining order. after stalking a woman for two years, including following her to Paris.

"My Lord, the Shana Grice Murder (2016), a case of profound tragedy, was a wakeup call to the way the police respond to stalking. The victim was not only stalked but murdered, bringing the limelight on the seriousness of stalking and why it has it be recognised as such. The perpetrator was sentenced to life imprisonment with a 25-year minimum.

"May I conclude with the Elliot Fogel case of 2022, my Lord! For 20 years, Fogel stalked Claire Waxman, which highlights the limitations of current legislation in cases where perpetrators breach lifetime restraining orders.

"It is in view of all that my Lord, that the state prays for a 10-year maximum imprisonment term for the accused, John Dube," Hachingson submitted.

Macdonald came through, and after a few rumblings in mitigation, concluded his final submissions. He knew the case had been lost, especially that the accused and already admitted. He only had to plead for a lighter sentence.

Chapter 31

The Dudula gang g, emboldened by public anger, expressed by mostly the poor, had taken their actions to the next level. Realising that Zimbabweans and other nationalities were no longer going to South African public hospitals, they changed tack. They worried that their campaign would soon fizzle out, thus they wanted something new to rekindle the raging fire against foreigners.

In Soweto, a group of the Dudula outfit was waiting purposefully at school gates. Something was brewing. Targeted at who? No one knew.

About 15 of them gathered at a bus terminus near a primary school in Soweto.

"Voetsek (get lost) Makwerekwere. Go back where you belong," ", they shouted, determinedly. . .

The South African Police Service (SAPS) was closely monitoring developments from their parked vehicles a short distance away. They knew how quickly the situation could escalate. S

The mob ordered parents of Zimbabwean learners to take their children home for good. They told them to immediately withdraw their children amid barrages of insults. The children had never seen such violence and hate before; hence they coiled in fear.

To them, school has always been credited as a place where leaders of tomorrow are raised and bred. But on that day, it was turned into something else; a place where the seeds of hate, discrimination, division, bitterness, strife and rivalry were sown; fertilised by violent chants and watered by tears.

The sight remained logged in their young memory. Just as South African youths suffered under apartheid, so were Zimbabweans and other foreigners, only that it was now at the behest of their fellow African brothers, whom they shared the trenches of struggle with. To them, it defeated logic that Africans could be called foreigners, worth of hate speech, violence and demeaning, in an independent South Africa.

It was such thinking, against the grain of Ubuntu, that Afrikaners watching from afar admired in the once-colonised blacks, using the same oppressive and separatist tactics against each other—straight from the colonialist's rulebook.

Nelson Mandela, Oliver Tambo, Walter Sisulu, Govan Mbeki, Thabo Mbeki, and other luminary freedom fighters who were jailed at Robben Island, would be disturbed by such happenings.

Perhaps the biggest disappointment came from JCM Zama's party, considering that JC, a freedom fighter, also spent years in detention at Robben Island, fighting for the black people's cause. He was now a central figure in the violent abuse of fellow blacks using apartheid-style tactics, even surpassing colonial masters at their game.

While colonial ill-treatment came mainly from men, South Africa gets the trophy for women empowerment. During colonial times, South African women fronted the struggle, reminding their husbands, fathers, brothers and sons to keep the fire of freedom burning.

In apartheid South Africa, the treatment of foreigners was strictly stratified by race and political utility, with white foreign nationals often welcomed or granted "honorary white" status. Conversely, foreign nationals of black African origin faced severe persecution, restricted rights, and potential deportation.

The South Africa of today appears to be reading from the same script. Fellow Africans are harassed and killed in violent xenophobic attacks.

Also, apartheid South Africa respected white foreigners and other non-black immigrants, glorifying them as investors. These were mostly from China, the United Kingdom, the Netherlands and the United States.

Black South Africans still revere whites, and disparage black foreigners in the same manner that Afrikaners treated them. Hence, their bitterness of the past is now misdirected at fellow black Africans, whom they consider the genesis of all problems. They forget that the unequal society created by colonialists, concentrating the bulk of the wealth in the hands of the minority white community, is what has impoverished them.

The colonial apparatus of oppression brutally punished revolutionary leaders across Africa, subjecting them to detention without trial, restrictions, torture and violence, which has somehow cascaded to the post-colonial state.

In South Africa, for example, black foreigners were often criminalised, imprisoned for minor offences, and, sometimes, summarily deported. The situation hasn't changed much. In fact, exploitation, particularly of migrants, has heightened. It is widespread in the agricultural sectors, where migrants are employed as menial labourers, often at low pay.

Chapter 32

"Have you reached a verdict yet?" Justice Lord Hamilton Lewis asked the jury at the Crown Court of England and Wales in the State vs John Dube case.

The question reverberated in John's mind, making him dizzy.

Jane Towers, the jury foreperson, stood up with a paper in her hand. She looked at Justice Lord Lewis, then turned her eyes on Hachingson, and finally settled them on John.

For the first time, since commencement of his trial, John felt a surge of confidence that even surprised him when he locked his eyes with juror Jane Towers'.

"Yes, my Lord, we have reached the verdict," replied the foreperson.

"Is your verdict partial or on accounts?" the judge asked.

"On all accounts my Lord," she replied.

"What is your verdict?" Justice Lord Lewis pressed on.

Her heart raced., She felt a strange pain in the gut, and her knees turned to jelly, almost giving in to an imminent fall. The court thought it was an act.

Regaining her composure at last, the foreperson, an eminent barrister in her own right, read out the verdict:

"We, the jury in State vs John Dube, have found the accused not guilty on both counts."

A deafening applause rose from the defence's corner. And an equally thunderous roar of disapproval erupted from the state's camp. There was commotion in the court, prompting John to head for the door, before the judge's proclamation. There were serious arguments from the jury's bench.

"Order in court," Justice Lord Lewis shouted, hitting the gavel.

Juror Jane Towers, the foreperson, collapsed. Within minutes sirens were heard outside the courtroom, followed by heavy thumping of feet.

First to barge in were two female medics in navy blue uniforms carrying a stretcher, and hard on their heels were six heavily armed policemen. In the melee, John attempted to bolt out, but he was tripped to the ground. Confusion ruled as everyone, including His Honour Justice Lord Lewis, scurried for cover.

"John Dube, you're under arrest for kidnapping Evelyn Towers, and holding her on ransom. You have the right to an attorney,", said a burly policeman pinning him down.

After regaining his composure, the judge hit the gavel, calling for everyone to sit down.

"Officer, do you realise that this is a superior court of law? How can you and your team storm in, just like that, reducing this honourable courtroom into a warzone and causing panic? I can charge you with contempt of court right away," Justice Lord Lewis fumed. "Without further ado, explain your actions."

"Good afternoon, Your Honour. My name is Chief Superintendent Noel Fitzgerald from the Anti-kidnapping and Extortion Unit. I am sorry to have stormed your court the way I did-" he attempted to explain.

"Son, you have a lot of explaining to do here," the judge interjected.

"We received information that Mrs Jane Towers, a jury foreperson in State vs John Dube, had her daughter, Miss Evelyn, kidnapped. Acting on that information, we conducted swift investigations. We established that Mrs Towers was being targeted to influence the decision of the jury in favour of the accused.. When he gathered that she won't play ball, he enlisted the services of a mafia trio to kidnap her little girl and held her for ransom to force compliance. A member of the gang went rogue and tipped off the police, leading to the arrest of the other two, who are assisting with investigations. John is alleged to be the leader of a drug trafficking syndicate," Chief Supt Fitzgerald explained.

Everyone in the courtroom was stunned. Events took a new twist. In shame, Macdonald left his client in the cold, declaring never to represent him again. Juror Jane Towers, who had earlier on swooned, had recovered through assistance from the right on time medics; and the jury had to retake its position on the case.

But before order returned, three more policemen arrived accompanied by Evelyn Towers, who identified John as the man who held her against her will.

Chief Superintendent Jones Fitzgerald and his team, including the new arrivals, took seats in the gallery, which was packed now as more journalists had joined, and waited for the resumption of the court session.

"Silence in court," the clerk of court announced.

Justice Lord Lewis took a glance at his wristwatch and cleared his throat.

"Members of the jury, you were still announcing your judgment when you were interrupted. Please proceed," he declared.

John froze.

"We, the jury in the case of State vs John Dube, have found the accused guilty on both counts," the foreperson announced, to an uproarious applause.

John felt a great wall collapsing on him. The judge looked at him thoughtfully.

"Since the defence counsel has unceremoniously withdrawn from the case, sentencing cannot proceed until the accused finds a lawyer to guide him in mitigation," he said.

"Proceedings may proceed, my Lord. I can represent myself," John said faintly.

"Son, are you aware that you cannot claim a mistrial on the basis of not having legal representation?" the judge asked.

"There is no need for that my Lord. I have nothing to say in mitigation. What I have is a complaint. In view of what has transpired earlier on, the position of the law is that a jury's verdict cannot be rescinded once declared in court. Since the jury announced a not guilty verdict on both cases, before the fracas, this court has no power, under whatever circumstances, to turn it, using whatsoever guise. The state would have to appeal the judgment. That's the law, Your Honour," John submitted.

"For a layman, your legal understanding is astounding," the judge remarked.

"I hold a Bachelor of Laws from the University of Wessex, my Lord, and am, therefore, not a layman," John said braggingly.

"Mr Dube, are you aware that the law allows the court to set aside any verdict when there is sufficient evidence of interfering with the jury," Justice Lord Lewis said.

"It may be so, my Lord. But how was the evidence of interference with the jury established? Considering your vast experience in the interpretation and upholding of the law, would you be swayed by hearsay? Which competent court of law has proven beyond reasonable doubt that there was, indeed, evidence of interference?" John asked confidently.

There were murmurs of approval in the gallery. The state counsel flinched, the jury foreman wiped her brows with the back of her right hand, and the judge fidgeted in his imposing hardwood and brown exotic leather chair.

"You have mastered the law my learned colleague," Justice Lord Lewis commended.

"The use of the word 'colleague' and the phrase 'learned colleague', while unharmful, tend to depict a picture of cajolement, which at law, is morally and ethically right. As a judge, you shouldn't be too familiar lest your reputation is brought into question," John cautioned the judge.

"Well, John, it was great exchanging legal opinion with you, but I am afraid, I must make a determination now," the judge said, adjusting his chair.

"John, I hereby sentence-" His Honour began.

"My Lord, the foreperson announced that I was found not guilty, hence, legally, I was exonerated from blame. The same foreperson, who announced a not guilty verdict, has no power to summarily retract it as she wishes on the basis of hearsay," John interrupted the judge.

"Speak again, and I will charge you with contempt of court," the judge threatened.

"Having been found guilty of stalking and harassment of Ms Sharon Tapfuma by a competent twelve-member jury, I hereby sentence you, John Dube, to ten years in prison; in solitary confinement. I hereby classify you as a dangerous criminal," Justice Lord Lewis ruled.

Ear-piercing ululations cut across the courtroom from the right corner of the gallery close to the entrance. It was from members of the International Coalition Against Abuse of Women. Sharon wept as scores of women embraced and consoled her.

A sea of camera flashes from the media section illuminated the courtroom as John was escorted by three prison guards to a waiting van to take him to prison.

Three days later, he was back in court facing kidnapping, drug trafficking and racketeering charges.

President Kufa was apprised by Ambassador Nyamapanga of the progress made in the case of Zimbabweans on death row in China. It was a difficult case to navigate.

The president had to personally go to China.

He arrived to a resounding welcome in Beijing at a ceremony attended by senior members of the Communist Party of China (CPC) and government officials. The ceremony was marked by the singing of Chinese and Zimbabwean national anthems, a 21-gun salute, and an inspection of the honour guard. President

Kufazvinei felt proud inspecting the guard of honour for the world's second largest economy.

Debate rages on whether China's military mighty is based on battle-tested equipment or is only derived from grandstanding parades and political posturing.

The welcome ceremony was followed by a cultural reception and banquet at the State Council hosted by President Xi. President Kufazvinei and his counterpart were welcomed by Chinese children waving flowers and flags. The children who perform on such occasions are well-trained and well-groomed. perform Their passion, energy and purposefulness reveal the ideologies of the people of China, and how this is instilled in young people from a tender age.

There was a closed-door meeting between the two heads of state, which touched on a number of issues, such as economic growth, food security, technology transfer, modernisation of critical infrastructure like airports, highways and power generation.

Finally, President Kufazvinei presented his case: "Your Excellence, there is a matter involving 200 of my people who have been sentenced to death for various offences. It is primarily for this issue that I'm here, knowing that China, a great all-weather friend of Zimbabwe, since the days of liberation struggle, will not abandon our longstanding ethos.

"I know how deeply you respect the rule of law as enshrined in the Constitution of the People's Republic of China. I have not come here to sway you from the position of the law, nor do I wish to lecture you on morality, no! My call isn't legal, although I'm aware that committing crimes in other countries constitute a breach of the law, which in my view is worth of reprimand. My request is premised on friendship and the sanctity of life. Please find it in your heart, my dear brother, my good friend, to let my people go."

"Your Excellence, please do not kneel before me. You are a man like me and a leader of your people, and I respect you for that," President Xi said.

"Kneeling down before you neither shows weakness nor lack of self-respect, Your Excellence. It shows how priceless my people are, and I know you have the power to pardon them," President Kufa said.

"I understand my brother, I sure do. That's the mark of a selfless leader and shepherd. I was formally informed of the issue. And, I must insist, China doesn't tolerant deviants. We respect the Constitution and it applies equally to everyone without fear or favour.

However, considering our great friendship, and as agreed by the CPC as a collective, I will grant only freedom to a hundred and fifty of them, including all women. The death penalty will not apply to all the remaining fifty. We may consider other options for some of them, depending on individual cases. We considered that freeing all the two hundred may send a wrong signal to would-be offenders," the Chinese president said. I

"Very well then," President Kufazvinei said elatedly. Although he would have wanted all the two hundred errant Zimbabweans pardoned, he knew that diplomatically, and with all women freed, he had scored big.

After the meeting, there was a press conference in which the two presidents spoke about the outcome. Negotiations on death row inmates were intentionally omitted.

President Kufazvinei and his delegation were showered with gifts. The Chinese people are known for their generosity. However, they are always thoughtful of the symbolism of the gifts and wrappers. They always avoid sets of four,, white wrapping paper wrapping (symbolising death), and sharp objects. Red and gold are preferred colours.

The president received a number of gifts that were never publicly disclosed.

Chapter 34

President Kufazvinei proclaimed the 4th of November as the day to commemorate the contribution of Zimbabweans living in the diaspora. The lobbying was done by Alex Chivandire, a US-based Zimbabwean, who had particularly taken interest in infrastructural developments in Zimbabwe.

The president was due to give a keynote address as the guest of honour at the Diaspora Day commemorations. The venue was Great Zimbabwe Monument in Masvingo.

In Zimbabwe, when a presidential event, such as a rally, project commissioning, or state visit, occurs at the provincial or district level, a hierarchical structure of government officials, security organs, and political party representatives coordinates to ensure its success. This process is highly centralised, with local officials acting on directives from the Office of the President and Cabinet (OPC).

Five weeks before the event, activities commenced and increased in momentum as the day drew closer. The military, police and Central Intelligence Organisation were working together at district , provincial and national levels. The Joint Operation Command held frequent meetings to discuss readiness from a security perspective. There was great anticipation as days passed.

Invitations had been sent to various ministries, embassies, the World Bank, International Monetary Fund, and Africa Development Bank, among other invited institutions and dignitaries.

"Ladies and gentlemen, we are all aware that His Excellence, President Kufazvinei will be attending the event. It is anticipated that many ambassadors and respected guests from the Bretton Wood Institutions will grace the event. We cannot afford to fail," said Charles Gidi, an intelligence operative for Harare.

"Thank you for your remarks, Cde Charles. as Masvingo Province, we're ready. The Minister of State for Provincial Affairs and Devolution is the highest political representative of the President in the province.

"In fact, our office is the office of the President at provincial level, and we hold overall responsibility for his visit, presiding over provincial state occasions, and monitoring the implementation of projects to be commissioned. So, everyone here is expected to follow our lead in the planning and execution of this event," said Catherine Tinarwo, from the Minister of State's office, gesturing with her hands at chest level.

There was momentary silence.

" Provincial Development Coordinator, I am sure you don't need reminding of your duties. Your role is to coordinate the logistics, liaise with the Office of the President and Cabinet, Protocol department, and ensure that all provincial heads of ministries align their actions with the presidential itinerary. I hope this is understood," Tinarwo added.

"The Provincial Security Committee made up of the police, army and the CIO, I want feedback regarding the security situation. This would specifically cover motorcade, venue safety, and clearance of the presidential team and VIPs. This task requires clinical precision. I want a readiness report regarding this matter as soon as possible," said Nelson Gwarada from the Office of the President and Cabinet.

"We are aware of our duties young man. You should never address us like that. Let that be the last time you talk to us like that," Brigadier-General Pfumo Jena said firmly and with finality.

There was tension in the room; the silence even scarier than the words uttered. When a person in authority speaks, it's always a good thing that they end with reassurances, regardless of their displeasure.

"May you please accept my apologies, Brigadier-General Jena and the military command here," Gwarada pleaded.

The brigadier-general nodded slightly, without saying anything.

Gwarada pretended to be unmoved by the power display, but the more he tried, the more it became evident that he was shaken to the core by the incident. He lost balance, his voice was now light, and he was unsure. He stole glances at all the people present; seeking approval, or at least assessing their reaction. He studied boy language for any familiar signs to the positive, but the miliary team wasn't compromising. They just stared at him, revealing nothing, sticking only to asked questions.

Looking directly at the brigadier-general, he said: "Turning to the District Development Coordinator (DDC), your role is to act as the head of administration at the district level. You're to coordinate all preparations, including logistics for the venue, infrastructure requirements, and communication with local stakeholders.

"This task requires meticulous planning and active stakeholder engagement, and project management skills. If you face any challenges, you may seek help," " Gwarada continued cautiously.

"Lewis, as the Rural District Council (RDC) chief executive officer, you and your technical staff of engineers and other professionals, should t prepare the venue, making sure it is accessible by grading roads, supplying water, setting up the tent and podium), as well as ensuring availability of ablution and sanitation facilities.

"The event is a state occasion, so all the line ministries and government departments are at your disposal. The Ministry of Local Government and Public Works, which your RDC falls under, and the Ministry of Transport and Infrastructural

Development, through the Rural Infrastructure Development Agency (RIDA), will assist you," Gwarada explained.

The provincial development coordinator, weighed in: "I also want to mention that traditional leaders should start mobilising their communities to attend the event and welcome the President, upholding the cultural decorum that we have always displayed on such occasions."

Resplendent in their traditional regalia and exuding power, chiefs Nyikadzino and Nemanwa were also in attendance.

"Lastly, I would like to remind the district security command of the police and CIO to remain vigilant. There should be meticulous traffic management, crowd control and intelligence gathering to curb disorder and ensuring a smooth running of the event," Gwarada concluded.

"The Minister of State for Provincial Affairs and Devolution, whom I represent, oversees the political and administrative aspects, While the District Development Coordinators and local authorities manage the technical, on-the-ground preparations. Security issues are handled by the Joint Operations Command (JOC) at both levels. We should work hand in glove to make this event a resounding success. This is our province; we have to make sure that we deliver without incident," a director from the minister's office said.

"Are there any questions?" Gwarada asked.

"Yes, sir! Who is responsible for accreditation of members of the media, and when is the process starting?" someone asked from the back of the room.

"That is under control, comrade," Gwarada answered reassuringly. "Any more questions?

Days and weeks following the meeting were marked by massive infrastructural developments with various agencies and departments working in sync. Work hastened as the big day approached—the day of commemorating the impactful contribution of the Zimbabwe diaspora towards the development of the motherland.

On Diasporans Day, the Harare-Beitbridge Highway and other roads and intersections leading to Great Zimbabwe Monument were heavily manned by the Zimbabwe Republic Police and other security personnel.

Desmond Chirongo Makate was the man tasked to plan the execution of "Assassinate President". His task was to design multiple possible ways in which the president could be assassinated and then provide solutions on tightening security. His report had been reviewed by the JOC and was approved as usual.

At State House, President Kufazvinei was preparing to leave.

"Daddy, are you going to leave without practicing your speech?" Melisa asked, winking playfully.

"Baby girl, what do you know about big people stuff"? This is presidential stuff, mind you. President Kufazvinei joked as he tickled his lastborn daughter.

She was adorable and challenged him all the time. Each time he wanted to feel like an ordinary citizen, he went to Melisa.

"Daddy, I have prepared a speech for you. You are to speak from the heart and that heart is me; I am your heart'; I want you to read only this script and no other. You will shine like a new penny," Melisa commanded, giggling and exposing a pair of dimples, which enhanced her beauty.

"I don't have time to read, baby girl; just fill me in, hey. What is it about? He cajoled her.

"Daddy, dearest; it's the wisdom of your fourth-grade daughter! Can you trust it to advance your career?" She replied with a question.

"Ok, then, impart the wisdom, my lovely girl," the president said, teasing her.

She screamed playfully and arranged the printed papers in her hand. Mimicking his hoarse voice, she read her prepared speech.

"Ladies and gentlemen, I your President, have heard your cries of distress, your agony and pain. The needless deaths, scornful treatment and the daily struggles you face have reached my heart. I am, therefore, offering a one-time offer for those in the diaspora willing to come back home. I will provide air tickets for those in the UK and buses for those in neighbouring countries. The Government has decided to bring back exiles facing hardships in neighbouring countries and overseas. We will offer three months free accommodation, farming land, and capital for them to start afresh back home.""

The Chief of Protocol and three other senior members of the ruling party, who had just entered, heard the girl fluently reading her speech. There was so much conviction in her voice. There was silent applause when she stopped. They were stunned.

Melisa's eyes dashed to the Chief of Protocol, then to his colleagues, and finally settled on her father.

"What wisdom we've here, my great advisor and-"the president praised, but Melissa caught him mid-sentence.

"Not so fast daddy! I called the Minister of Finance and asked her if she would support such a proposal. And she said she would ask her team to do some computations to see if that were possible.

"I reminded her of how we effectively responded to Covid-19, which means our readiness to accommodate our people in the diaspora. And, besides, we have the land," she explained.

"Your Excellence, I am speechless. Such wisdom from a Grade Four pupil is astounding. Please consider her advice. She makes a lot of sense, Mr President, encourage her," the Chief of Protocol said.

"Sydney, I know you are only saying this because she is my daughter. That's what's clouding your judgement. Be factual in your review of this. This has to go through an inter-ministerial taskforce as is norm, before any decision can be made. I know you're aware of that, Sydney," the president said sternly.

"Darling, don't tell me your gentlemen here are considering implementing suggestions from a fourth-grade learner," into national business," Mrs Aquilia Kufa, the first lady, remarked in apparent disregard to Melisa's feelings.

President Kufa was heartbroken. He followed Melisa to her room. She had locked herself in and when he knocked there was no response.

"Little angel, little angel, little angel, let me in..." President Kufa sang. She eventually opened the door, allowing him in, giggling.

He looked around the room. It was decorated in pick; everything was pink. There was order. No litter. Nothing was out of place.

"Lisa darling, something about your proposal caught my attention. May you kindly allow me to incorporate it into my speech? He asked politely.

The president was elated but as he left his daughter's bedroom. But as he stepped out into the corridor, Melisa gently cleared her throat. Remembering something, he turned back. He lifted her up and gave her a strong hug.

"Your Excellence, sir! We leave in ten minutes," a member of his team said firmly yet respectfully.

He walked to his official ZIM 1 Mercedes Benz, a symbol of national pride and an embodiment of self-rule, accompanied by the first lady.

The motorcade comprised police outriders blaring sirens, clearing the way, more than thirty huge fuel guzzlers, three military Toyota Land Cruisers each with at least 12 well-trained commandoes armed to the teeth, five police Mercedes Benz vehicles, a jammer vehicle, and two ambulances. The usually congested Tongogara Avenue was cleared in no time as the Head of State and Government, Commander-in-Chief of the Zimbabwe Defence Forces, Chancellor of all State universities and First Secretary of the ruling party, His Excellence, Dr Kufazvinei Matambudziko's motorcade passed at high speed. It was such an awesome spectacle. The first lady particularly loved that demonstration of power.

The jammer vehicle was a recent addition to President Kufazvinei Matambudziko's motorcade. It is crucial in that remote-controlled improvised explosive devices (RCIED) pose a real threat to VIP convoys. A convoy jammer vehicle is a 4×4 car equipped with a jamming system that can block a wide range of radio frequency (RF) communications, cellular and satellite communications, in order to prevent activation of RCIEDs.

The jammer vehicle is engineered to provide maximum protection by establishing a secure electronic shield that blocks wireless receivers from being remotely triggered. It features a self-sustaining battery bank supported by a specially upgraded alternator and an advanced heat dissipation system. The vehicle can operate by jamming either the full frequency spectrum or specific selected frequency bands. Fitted with omnidirectional antennas, it delivers comprehensive 360-degree coverage, includes full climate control, and has been developed from practical real-world   operational experience.

The motorcade cruised into Rotten Row, struggling around potholes just after crossing Robert Mugabe Way. It raced to the Mbare Flyover and spectacularly circled into Simon Mazorodze Road. It was such a sight. Many surreptitiously took videos, as it was against the law, but also knowing the head it created for the place, as they would have to arrest an entire street.

The convoy approached the Zimbabwe Broadcasting Corporation Mbare Studios, as it raced towards Manchester Road, Zindoga shops in Waterfalls, and the newly constructed Trabablas Interchange at the intersection of Simon Mazorodze, Chitungwiza, and High Glen roads.

Suddenly, the radio communication system came alive.

"Look inside gentlemen, the President wants to do the thing," one commander yelled.

"Tango one, what the hell is the thing?" one biker asked.

"Alpha Mike, the President wants to circle Trabablas. Make it happen, gentlemen," he replied.

"Negative, another time; the distance is too short. We will cause confusion; security on the ground is not aware," the lead yelled in disagreement.

"Raptor, this is an order".

And, so it was. The convoy circled the Trabablas Interchange twice.

"Wow! Look at that, babe. This is one of the most sophisticated interchanges in Africa. There are a few that can compete with this mighty one," President Kufazvinei said proudly.

"Babe, you know what? I am not happy with the way you take sides with Melisa. I am your wife, and the only first lady, yet you side with her. You listen to her. I have also noted the way you embrace her. It's like you have a deep desire to always hold her. Why not have that same thing for me," The first lady complained, ruining what should have been a spectacular view of the interchange named after an eminent revolutionary, whose liberation struggle moniker was Trabablas Dzokerai Mabhunu.

"Darling, you cannot be serious, really. Melisa is your daughter. How can you be jealous of your daughter?" The president asked, hardly hiding his displeasure.

"As long as she is interfering between me and my man, I am not backing off," she said tersely.

"What exactly did she disturb this time around, if I may ask?" The president asked.

"I wanted one for the road and you wouldn't give me. I kept calling you, and I even sent you messages on your phone, but you were too busy to read the messages," The first lady said hurtfully.

The president, ashamed of the nugget of information shared, looked around to determine if the driver had heard anything, but there was no way to tell. Chauffeurs are trained not to hear, comment or interfere in any way, unless spoken to. They focus mainly on their job.

He lowered his head and whispered into her ears: "I will give you today after the event and meetings."

"So, babe how do you want me. I want to get dirty tonight," the first lady whispered.

The motorcade passed the Skyline Tollgate, as it raced towards Beatrice where one of the most decorated generals of the army and a stalwart of the liberation struggle died in an inferno at his farm. He had died in a manner that brought many questions than answers.

They went past Chivhu. The president asked his team to stop at market stall along the highway where he wanted to buy sweet potatoes. He did not alight from the vehicle after the security team advised him against the idea.

On arrival at the venue, the president was briefed by the Minister of State for Provincial Affairs and Devolution on activities in Masvingo Province. At 11.45am he took to the podium to address delegates.

After observing all the protocol, the president delivered his keynote address.

"Fellow Zimbabweans, I address you on this historic day when we commemorate the contribution of our diaspora compatriots. My government is aware of the immense contributions being made by Zimbabweans living in the diaspora. I have taken steps to ensure that their efforts will not go unnoticed.

Fellow, Zimbabweans, our people in the diaspora are making significant, transformative contributions across diverse economic sectors in the country. Their impact is felt in both their host countries and in the economic, social, and infrastructural development of our great country, Zimbabwe.

"Our country boasts of a high literacy rate, and a strong, skilled, and professional populace. They are driving innovation, entrepreneurship, and financial initiatives, making Zimbabwe a major exporter of talent to many countries. He, the nation is benefiting from these immense contributions.

"Fellow Zimbabweans, on the economic front, our country has received significant financial inflows. The diaspora has become a vital lifeline for Zimbabwe. Diasporans look after their relatives and invest in income-generating projects back home, with remittances reaching nearly US$2,6 billion in 2024 and projected to go higher in 2025/2026.

"These funds account for roughly twelve percent of Zimbabwe's gross domestic product (GDP). Furthermore, diasporans have contributed to the fast growth we have witnessed in the real estate sector, especially in residential property development. There has been significant downstream effect on the tourism subsector, as they boast the aviation business due to increased flights. Two major airlines are now overwhelmed with bookings and are always fully booked on their London-South Africa route.

"These remittance sources come from our two major labour export markets, led by South Africa and followed by the United Kingdom, which largely employs professionals like accountants, engineers, teachers, and doctors, among others. The UK has recently overtaken South Africa as the top source of remittances, accounting for, approximately 28.6 percent of inflows. This highlights the global spread of Zimbabwean professionals. There has been a steady number of Zimbabweans leaving for Canada, the United States and the United Arab Emirates, but their contributions are still to be recognised.

"Fellow Zimbabweans, as I alluded to earlier, diasporans are making lifechanging investments in Zimbabwe, which go beyond supporting families. They are investing in real estate, solar-powered farms, schools, and healthcare facilities, acting as a crucial force for national rebuilding. As you may all be aware of, our great country was ravaged by illegal criminal and unwarranted economic sanctions imposed by Britain and its allies following the post-2000 Fast Track Land Reform Programme aimed at empowering our people through landownership.

"The more than two decades of evil economic assault on our people created a national housing backlog of between 1,2 million and two million units. Hence, the diaspora community should be appreciated for their contribution towards closing this gap. Mortgage finance has largely been unavailable, creating a dry and illiquid real estate market. To that end, my government pays tribute to Zimbabweans living in the diaspora.

"Fellow Zimbabweans, our dedicated investment in both primary, secondary and tertiary education has created high-level professionals able to deliver creative excellence at their workplaces. Thus, our people have become sought-after professionals across the world. The technical and professional training rooted in deep professionalism and uncompromised work ethic anchored in Ubuntu/Hunhu has made our people rise and be counted, even in foreign soils.

Ladies and gentlemen, allow me to express my heartfelt and profound gratitude to our diaspora community across oceans and seas, and indeed, those closer to our beautiful country. These Zimbabweans have become the source of joy and happiness for thousands of families. Furthermore, the downstream effect in tax revenue from Value Added Tax (VAT), Sugar Tax and Intermediated Transfer Tax on transactions, to Capital Gains Tax when they transfer their properties through conveyancing processes, has been astronomical.

"My government recognises the black tax that Zimbabweans in the diaspora are paying, the kindness of looking after their extended families, with each Zimbabwean in the diaspora looking after at least twenty-five to thirty people directly and indirectly. Families have been uplifted through investments in self-help projects, such as poultry, piggery and farming in general. Though I have a bone to chew with some of you here; be they parents, brothers or sisters, who have been defrauding those living in the diaspora.

"You hear someone with a toothache requiring a simple extraction that costs less than US$15 at our healthcare facilities across the country, communicating it as a root canal procedure, which they say costs US$1 200. Some of you are receiving money pretending to be building houses and doing home improvements, but you are not. A lot of you are threatening those in the diaspora with silent treatment if they do not send you money immediately when you ask for it.

"People in the diaspora are working hard; doing three to four shifts to make ends meet. They do not rest, yet *imi murikuto fadaya zvenyu kuno vamwe vachibhenda chasi* (you are busy enjoying life while others toil).

"Fellow Zimbabweans, the United Kingdom has benefited from our learned and professional hardworking people, who have transformed service delivery in healthcare and specialised care. Many Zimbabweans hold significant positions in the UK's National Health Service (NHS), Australia, and Canada, particularly as nurses and carers. We are deeply indebted to those professionals for lifting the Zimbabwean flag higher.

"On the global stage, we have our very own Zimbabwean artists making waves. These Zimbabweans have demonstrated immense talent and are counted among some of the best talent in global entertainment and arts, with figures such as Rachel Chinouriri, Munashe Chirisa, Leostaytrill, and S1mba making waves. Our people have received recognition under platforms like the Zimbabwe Achievers Awards, spearheaded by figures like Conrad Mwanza.

"Many Zimbabweans have established businesses in host countries that facilitate trade with Zimbabwe, helping to import essential goods. This has become a reference point in nation-building as we move towards increasing trade with many countries that had placed illegal sanctions against our beautiful country. We have seen increased participation in the diaspora investments roadshow. Please come and invest back home.

"Fellow Zimbabweans, notwithstanding the impressive record as I have alluded to earlier, my heart is deeply saddened by the suffering that our people are going through in many countries across the world. We have our children trapped in unforgiving foreign prisons; our brothers and sister are tortured and discriminated against in different countries. I have received disturbing statistics that even innocent schoolchildren are discriminated against. They are withdrawn from school and treated like criminals. It has come to my attention that even hospitals are no longer allowed to take in foreign nationals. Their distress call has reached my heart. I have, therefore, tasked the Minister of Public Service, Labour and Social Welfare , Minister of Local Government and Public Works and the Minister of Primary and Secondary Education to intervene. We discussed the need for a broader framework for the repatriation of our people.

"As your listening servant leader, I cannot watch while our own people are treated with contempt. I thank you."

The president's speech was received with thunderous applause amid drumming, ululations, whistling and singing.

Chapter 35

On the sidelines of the inaugural Diasporans Day celebrations held at Great Zimbabwe Monument in Masvingo, a journalist, Nomagugu Ndlovu from Zimpress was interviewing some of the people at the event. And the first to be interviewed was Dorothy Chauke.

"A very packed message from His Excellence, President Kufazvinei; what is your key take away from it?" Nomagugu asked.

"Well, the president has hit the nail on the head. He demonstrated understanding of the economic impact of contributions from those living in the diaspora. He came with credible numbers to support his speech, something we hadn't seen his predecessors doing." Dorothy responded.

"You talked about supporting the speech with evidence. What specifically did you like about the president's speech today?" Nomagugu followed up with another question.

"The president mentioned housing projects being done by Zimbabweans in the diaspora. These investments have resulted in the significant growth of the real estate sector. He also touched on tax revenue contributions from VAT to Capital Gains Tax and a number of other taxes," Dorothy explained.

"Very specific, indeed," Nomagugu acknowledged, turning to a bespectacled delegate. "Coming to you, Professor Letwin Sambo; the issues raised by the president seem to show the role being played by those in the diaspora in nation building. Do you think there is, perhaps, a need to recognise these people in a much more meaningful way than just a day to commemorate them?"

"Thank you so much, Nomagugu, for giving me this opportunity. I think the president has had a good start. He articulated the housing contribution that was mentioned by the previous interviewee, the tax revenue and the Consolidated Revenue Fund or CRF for short. The president mentioned the social impact anchored on Ubuntu/Hunhu as diasporans provide for their extended families. This is the hallmark of true Africanism.

"The president surprised everyone when he raised the issue of xenophobic attacks on our people in South Africa, where many have been killed and injured. The proposal by the president to offer those who want to come back home a chance to do so is a welcome development," Prof Sango said.

"Following up on that, Prof, What do you make of the proposed repatriation of the exiles? Do you believe the country has adequate financial resources and the administrative capacity to do so?" Nomagugu asked.

"That's a valid question Nomagugu. I believe there is a plan being worked out by the relevant ministries to bring this proposal to fruition. I believe, at this stage, it might be too early to comment on the viability of the plan. As I see it, it will be implemented based on recommendations from the envisaged inter-ministerial taskforce," she said.

"Before you go, Prof, what is your take on the voters' rights of Zimbabweans based in the diaspora? Nomagugu asked?

"Well, Zimbabweans living in the diaspora are citizens of Zimbabwe. In my view, they have the right to determine who governs their country given their significant contribution to the nation as enunciated by His Excellence, the President," Prof Sango said.

Melisa was watching all the proceedings and she was satisfied that she had influenced national policy, but she knew that she had booked a match with her mother. The first lady was not one to let go things easily, especially where it involved her man.

Done with proceeding at the event, the president prepared to leave.

"Babe, I am tired. I want to use a helicopter. I don't want to go by road. In any case, you owe me a good time; we agreed. No more meetings today," the first lady said, clasping her hand into his.

"Darling, calm down, please. This isn't the right time to talk about sex," the president whispered in her ear.

"Look here, my love; you see all these people? Come nighttime they will be all tucked in their bedrooms cuddling their spouses and satiating each other's sexual desires. And today, we are going to do exactly that," she read him rule number one of matrimony.

The president looked at her, then blankly stared into space pondering an alternative to a get reprieve from his wife for the night ahead.

"Your Excellence, sir! The helicopter is ready. We will be leaving in twenty minutes," an aide informed the president.

The "thing" was performed again on the return journey. The helicopter circled Trabablas Interchange thrice before heading straight to State House.

Chapter 36

It was on Christmas Eve that the South African National Defence Force intercepted 1174 undocumented Zimbabweans attempting to cross into South Africa using the Limpopo River.

A long and winding queue of illegal immigrants, among them, children and women with babies strapped on their backs was led to holding camps in the Limpopo province. The fact that children are often carried with no documentation has sparked debates on possible kidnapping, trafficking of young boys into slavery or girls into either forced marriages or prostitution.

The South African Police Service and the military immediately called for assistance in setting up camps to detain the scores of illegal immigrants. Once intercepted by SANDF patrols, undocumented migrants were handed over to immigration officials under South Africa's Border Management Authority (BMA). From there, they were screened, documented, and held briefly at processing or holding facilities before deportation arrangements were made.

Meanwhile, Melisa was in her bedroom in the west wing of the president's residence at State House, watching a South African news channel, when a video clip appeared showing scores of Zimbabweans being rounded up for attempting to cross into South Africa illegally. Touched, she decided to reach out to some very important people.

"Good afternoon, ma'am! My name is Melisa. May I please talk to the Minister of Foreign Affairs! It's urgent", she said in polite but urgent voice.

"Good afternoon, ma'am. Where exactly are you calling from?" the lady on the other end asked dismissively, concluding that it was possibly a child playing with the phone.

"I am a Zimbabwean citizen, which qualifies me to engage any public official who works for the Government of Zimbabwe. Is that not so ma'am? She asked assertively.

"Hold on, please."

There was a moment of silence as the lady on the other end was possibly consulting.

"Prof, there is a girl on the line. I have put her on hold. She wants to talk to you. She said her name is Melisa," Nomsa explained.

"The only friend I know whose name is Melisa is the president's daughter. But she has never called me using the office numbers. We always talk whenever I visit the State House. Anyway, just let her through," the minister said.

"Good afternoon, Melisa! I am Professor-" she greeted.

"Oh, my friend," Melisa interrupted her, "how are you? Do you have a TV in your office? Yes, you do; please tune in to SABC News, right away".

The minister was horrified to see many Zimbabweans crossing the Limpopo River, taking risky manoeuvres. Scores of others already on the South African side were being directed into holding zones escorted by heavily armed soldiers. His heart sank.

"Prof, are you there? Melisa asked urgently. What do you say about this? For how long can we watch while our people, our flesh and blood, take risks like that"? Are you sure nothing can be done about it?" Melisa poured her heart out.

"I will look into it, my friend," the minister said reassuringly.

Later that day, Melisa confronted her father.

"Mr President, as a citizen of Zimbabwe, my heart is deeply moved by the way our people are suffering in South Africa," she complained.

"Come on, darling. Don't be too emotional," President Kufazvinei consoled her, adding, "Well, suppose you are given a chance to be the president of this beautiful country, what would be your solutions? I'm giving you five minutes."

"Well, sir, we can start by reviving all the facilities we used for returnees during Covid-19. We will work with local authorities to assess the schools and other council facilities to ensure that there is capacity to receive, process and assist those coming back from South Africa.

"Regarding transportation, we have a government-to-government programme similar to the one between Nigeria and South Africa. The Nigerian government provided planes while Malawi provided buses to transport their people back home.

"Now, our people want good healthcare services, employment and better living conditions for them to stay home. I do not see the reason why we should fail to deliver that. Our country has vast natural resources and a ban on export of raw minerals will attract significant investments in manufacturing, thus creating hundreds of thousands of jobs here," Melisa explained.

"Well done, Madam President. So, how do you intend to deal with attracting investors to Zimbabwe? We are not the only investment destination, remember," the president said.

"Well, there are many ways of dealing with that. We can reduce business license processing times, cut down on licensing fees, reduce corporate tax, and payroll taxes," Melisa proposed.

"But this will reduce government revenue. How then would you fund your annual national budget? President Kufazvinei asked.

"Your Excellence, sir, you need a wider tax base to have more tax income. Do you realise that the sanctions imposed on our country by the US and EU have resulted in the closure of more than a thousand companies? Encouraging investments in manufacturing is the way to go. Lower taxes and easing the way business is done will lead to the creation of more jobs, hence widening the tax base. Value addition will also create additional export revenue and generate more foreign currency," Melisa said as if possessed.

"I am impressed, Madam President. But, tell me, is this what they are now teaching you in primary school? There seem to be much better teaching at school these days than it was during our time?" the president admitted.

The future was indeed in safe hands.

"Oh, daddy. Don't flatter me. So, are we together on this? she asked, smiling.

"I can't promise. I've to discuss this with the Minister of Foreign Affairs and get views from the Minister of Finance and Minister of Local Government," the president said.

"Well, since you are the president, you can talk to them. But I have already briefed them. They have given me their word that if the instruction comes from the president himself, they will be willing to act on it. So, the ball is in your court now Mr President," Melisa informed him.

"Looks like you have the confidence to talk to big people. I will have a discussion with them and see what I can do," The president said reassuringly.

At 8pm the following day the president appeared on national television. It was a presidential emergency address.

"Fellow Zimbabweans, my government has taken notice of the suffering of our people in various countries across the globe. As such, we have reactivated our Covid-19 response mechanisms. Thus, all the facilities used during the pandemic as quarantine and isolation centres for people coming from various countries are being readied to receive our people. Everything is also being done to give them a safe landing as they settle in," President Kufazvinei said.

By midnight the news was trending on all major international news feeds and social media platforms.

Farai, Gabriel and Takudzwa, were among the more than three million Zimbabweans in the diaspora, who received the news with much anticipation.

Chapter 37

Sharon was mentally tired when she met Roland Adams of Swedish British nationality in a London shop. She looked all dejected and unhappy.

"Hey beautiful. You don't look happy. What's the matter?" Roland asked.

Sharon rolled up her eyes in a "whatever dude" way. But this did little to upset Roland Adams.

"And if I am unhappy, I suppose you're the guy with the antidote?" Sharon asked sarcastically.

"See, I am already having an effect on you. If I spend an hour with you, you will forget all your worries," Roland said.

"Wow! Looks like we have a guy who thinks too much of himself here. And I am not really in the mood. If I had time, I would have shown you that none of your antics really works," Sharon said disinterestedly.

"Well, this man is like race car—never seen a set of tail-lights after asking for a girl's number. Never," Adams replied confidently, head held high, revealing his Adam's apple.

"Really? I can't believe what I am hearing. So, you think you are going to walk away with my number, right?" Sharon replied in annoyance.

"You're just hiding behind that false macho bravado. I will shake off that wall, and when that happens, not only will I walk away with your number, but I will also walk away with everything; precisely with you, honey,"" Adams said.

"I noticed your loneliness and sadness, that's why I wanted to put a smile on your face," Adams added.

He pulled out a white handkerchief from his jacket pocket and wiped a teardrop from Sharon's left eye, which she had attempted to conceal. She wanted to pull away, but she remained transfixed at the spot, unable to move away from him.

Admiring his chiselled chest and biceps, she got carried away into wonderland. She imagined herself locked in his powerful arms. And, like the knowledgeable say, the rest was history.

* * *

After the court cases, Sharon, Roland Adams and Nancy decided to visit Dubai, a city and emirate in the United Arab Emirates, for a holiday. The idea was to rest, refresh and recharge.

At the Nathan Towers, Sharon and Roland were staying in the 13th floor. Their room was luxurious. Their 7-star hotel room was designed for ultimate luxury, with a number of high-quality materials from China, Italy and Africa, precisely Zimbabwe. the room featured expansive layouts with panoramic views created for extreme luxury, tailormade furniture, and smart home automation.

The rooms at the hotel also featured two king-size beds with high-thread-count linens, private balconies overlooking the city of peace, as it is popularly known for, exuding futuristic experiences decades ahead. There was a jacuzzi, and opulent materials, like marble, silk, and wood veneers—all designed to thrill and offer an unforgettable lifetime experience.

These spaces were characterised by meticulous attention to detail exhibiting exceptional craftsmanship. The ambient lighting illuminated the vast space creating a heavenly feeling. The in-room artificial intelligence-enabled technology read temperatures and could make adjustments when needed. Hanging on the walls were mostly Italian and French collections of curated art.

Nancy occupied a spacious and luxurious one-bedroomed apartment. She was joined by her boyfriend who flew all the way from Zimbabwe to see her.

The first day was eventful. The four went to the Aquarium, then visited the Burj Khalifa, the world's tallest building.

The following day was, a Sunday, started off as a normal day with travellers paying little attention to the hostilities between the US, Israel and Iran. The four were playing all sorts of games and enjoying themselves experimenting with food like everyone else.

On the 28th of February 2026, the US and Israel waged a war against Iran. Nancy, Sharon and their boyfriends were caught unaware. What started as a triangular conflict involving three countries, soon spread like a veld fire, engulfing the entire Middle East, creating a no-fly zone. Initially, Iran retaliated by attacking US bases in the region. Sensing danger, all major airlines cancelled their flights.

By day three, foreign countries had decided to evacuate their nationals from the Middle East for safety reasons. International news agencies covered the events as they developed.

"Sharon, my dear; what do we do now? We alerted the embassy of our presence here, and processes to evacuate us have begun. My worry now is Nathan, my Zimbabwean boyfriend. He doesn't have a British visa. I'm afraid that if we leave him here, he will be stranded," Nancy said.

"Nancy dear, we should take it one day at a time. Let's leave this in the hands of God. Here, there are so many variables at play, and we cannot plan under such circumstances. We can only manage the situation as it comes," Sharon reasoned.

"Maybe we should enquire from the British Embassy if they can consider your man's plight, since he is in the company of legitimate citizens," Roland weighed in.

"Guys don't worry about me. I can take care of myself. I have a plan in mind," Nathan said thoughtfully.

Impossible as it seemed, the following day Nathan boarded a bus bound for Saudi Arabia. While the airspace was closed, there was limited road access for those who wanted to leave Dubai.

By day three, Nathan was in Jordan. He managed to connect directly with the Foreign Affairs ministry and negotiations for his passage were done ahead of his travel. From Jordan's Al Aqubah, he flew to Egypt, then to Ethiopia. By day five, he was on his way to Zimbabwe.

The other three were trapped in Dubai. There were further bombings at the airport, further dampening their hopes of evacuation. There was a glimmer of hope, though, when the President of Iran appeared to offer apologies regarding the bombing of neighbouring countries. However, this hope soon faded. It was realised that the president was a ceremonial figure in Iran, and that, at the time, the Islamic Revolutionary Guard Corps (IRGCS) was in charge of military operations.

Turn the page for an exclusive sneak peek at the next book!

The gods Above

A Religious Thriller

Elliot Chatima and Rumbi Chen

Chapter 1

It was a cool Thursday morning with a patchy morning drizzle, light thunder showers expected later in the day, according to the MET department. Time really moves fast, the days are fleeting, the sound of New Year celebrations and the memories of Christmas cheer, partying and the bullet sound of firecrackers were still echoing in our ears and yet we were already in the month of April. Noel Kasamba was having a glass of Amarula mixed with Ultra Heat Treated (UHT) milk, a mix only for the lactose tolerant. He was holding a giant marijuana cigarette, which made choking smokes for those not used to such strong "medicine". Noel was a man with seven wives and 28 children. He had married the women simultaneously when they were between the ages of 10 and 13. He had lost three wives and 3 children due to pregnancy and birth complications.

Susan, his first wife, was now 25 and a mother of 5 children. Each woman had been given a field measuring one hectare to cultivate with her children. In that sort of work; numbers mattered and the wife with many children had a lighter burden.

Susan entered Noel's chambers. She knelt before him and waited for him to speak. Noel cleared his throat and looked aside as if checking if anyone was coming. He licked his lips, lubricating his mouth with saliva, looking at Susan intently and started, "You know my heart beats for you, right? There can be nothing difficult for me to do for a queen like you. You are my number one girl here."

Susan looked at Noel and started giggling like a little girl. "If you say so. There are times I begin to think that you have forgotten about me. These new girls keep you busy these days and you have forgotten about me," she complained. "I am your first love. When I first met you we both had never married. I was young. How I wish things could have remained the same way," she continued.

"So you are still dreaming of the two of us only?" Noel demanded

Susan looked at him. "You know how we were so pristine and we knew nothing about making love. I had to research a lot and it was great to see how much progress we made and when I was beginning to think that we were getting the hang of it, then boom - another woman."

Noel moved closer to her, trying to bring her closer with his right hand but Susan was chocked by the smoke from the marijuana. She backed off and Noel laughed as he made aggressive pulls of the marijuana cigarette before coughing and releasing smoke into the air. He made two quick sips of Amarula before he spoke. "Pardon my bad manners, you requested to see me? What is it?"

Susan cleared her throat, looked at Noel as if trying to gauge his mood before she spoke. "My Lord," she started "Angela your seventh wife is heavily pregnant and from our assessment, we believe she will not be able to deliver the baby in a normal way. We think it's a great idea to take her to the hospital."

Noel erupted from the bed and like a possessed man grabbed Susan by the throat and began to chock her then threw her to the couch, narrowly missing the wall. He looked at Susan for a moment before he spoke. "The next time you speak to me like that you will not be so lucky. I will kill you and I will kill you dead." Noel was shaking with anger. He was failing to control himself and in the end he sat down. There was complete silence. The Silence was broken by a loud cry from the other room. They looked at each other before Noel shouted "go and look at it and manage the situation, even if the baby is crossing, she will deliver the same way others have. She will deliver here. Call the lady from the next compound."

There was commotion in the next three hours that followed, Angela was given a homemade concoction to take, and it was a traditional mixture meant to induce a baby to come. After taking it, Angela started sweating and shaking. The other three of Noel's wives were holding her while the other one was wiping the sweat and calming her down. The screams were loud, a call for help. She called her father and mother in desperate plea to seek help. The screams were sharp and disturbing even the elderly midwife asked that Angela be taken to the hospital but that was a non-starter. Angela had got married at the age of 12 and at 13 when she was pregnant. There was an unwritten law amongst the community of "believers" that women will give birth at home and will never go for weighing scale or for vaccination. The idea was to evade jail and prison was not far.

Angela screamed one more time and pushed and pushed. It was clear she wanted the baby to come out thus she used all the force she had but to no avail. Everyone watched as she began to grow tired and powerless. Susan ran to Noel to alert him but he was not in the mood. He did not entertain her.

Susan ran to Angela, raised her head and appealed to her to push one more time. "You can do it my friend, please don't give up." Susan urged her. Angela summoned all the power and spoke. "I think my baby has crossed, they are not coming. I am tired, I am leaving you and my body is getting cold. Tell my father that I love him and that I forgive him for what he did to me, cutting my life at a developmental stage and handing me over to be raped daily and left to die. Please make sure that you will treat your girls with dignity and that they will go to school." Angela looked at Susan while the midwife cast a lone and disturbed figure. She wrestled with thoughts and she did not realise that she was talking loudly and all the debate in her heart she aired out.

Angela looked at Susan, "I want to go Vakoma (Sister) I need you to promise me. I need you to avenge my death." At that point everyone noticed that Lucia was in the room. Because of the commotion, no one had noticed and she saw and heard everything. Angela looked at Lucia and with a weak hand gesture she called her close. "Lucia my baby, I am dying. You know and have seen what I went through. I need you to remember me and protect your sisters." She pleaded with her. At that point Lucia was afraid and started screaming and went out. She ran away from home and was never seen again.

Back to the room Angela breathed her last.

Angela's parents were informed and the following morning she was buried in a shallow grave in the compound. She was buried in an unmarked grave, wrapped in a reed mat with a plastic on top and trees were planted on top of the grave.

Susan had nightmares the few days that followed. Noel realised that his women were disturbed and called them. "I know what happened here has traumatized you, I could have addressed you before. The spirit had shown me that the evil one shall come and will sit in the midst of the family and bring foreign ideas, but I prayed that none of that should happen. Angela was used by the devil and her death is a defeat to the powers of darkness. We have conquered," Noel charged. All the women looked at Susan for approval and what Susan approved, everybody would follow without question.

Susan had not gone to school but she was intelligent. She had mastered the art of deception but she still had flaws as an uneducated person and her skimming would actually be foisted. Susan looked at everyone and looked at Noel who was now portraying a face of a hungry puppy begging for food. She looked down and clinked her fist and closed her eyes as she presumably tried to shake off the loud creams and the plea for help by Angela from her mind. In the end tears flowed effortlessly and when she spoke, her voice was low but audible.

"Indeed as our father and husband has said, we were under attack by the evil spirit. This event, the death of Angela, was Satan's doing and we must be united and pray that the evil departs from this house and from our lives forever." When she was done talking, she was shaking and her teeth gritted. All the other women responded with an "Amen" but Noel was not to be fooled. She saw the pain and trauma in Susan.

The following day Noel and his six wives prepared for church. It was a Passover meeting and they were going to be gone for six days. They were part of the Mission Critical Church of Apostles. The name sounded like a government department responsible for espionage and other secretive missions. But that did not matter because the church had existed for 85 years.

The members wore blue uniforms and white from time to time. They camped in Buhera and instantly the place became a business hub. Women were responsible for making food, provide hot water for their husbands and making tea as and when it was needed.

Noel was a high ranking member who sat in the council of the church's leadership. They each took turns to preach to their congregants. The sitting arrangement was wired. The men sat in front facing young girls while and the boys sat behind their fathers, while the mothers sat behind their daughters.

A time of prophecy came and all the leaders started speaking in tongues, *"Hiririririri CD Ramachksaakada aaaaa bullshit yematatya."*

The first one to speak was the leader of the church and there would be a second person to repeat what the leader would have said. "The spirit has shown me a family that will perish tonight but there is nothing to fear as all has been revealed to me." This, he said to wild cheers. The congregants were aware of what was about to happen. "The Spirit has said unto me, that if I take the daughter in marriage, the death will be averted and the entire family will be saved from harm." He continued. He looked at the young girls, barely 12 years and pointed at one of them and asked her to stand up. The family approached the leader and knelt before him. They grabbed their daughter by the hand and without emotion or question, they handed her over. There were loud cheers and applause with women immediately erupting into songs of "praise and worship." The act was considered sent by God.

Next was Noel, he had taken Marijuana and his famous Amarula his tongues were a border line circus and in the end he too prophesied. "Zvanzi nemweya (The spirit said) there is a girl sitting in front of you, that girl, you are to pray for her and she will be promiscuous, sorry meant prosperous, she must come to you." Mothers urged their children to run and the one that came to him was the one he wanted, he had stood right in front of her. When the girls stood before him, he continued, "The spirit said you shall bear fruit and be wealthy and prosperous in my house. You shall be my wife from today." The young girl was shocked and she attempted to run away but her parents grabbed her and handed her over to Noel. Susan looked at the scene and Noel cast a gaze in her direction, as if to show that he was the man and did whatever he wanted.

Noel had taken another "wife" a thirteen year old girl. The girl shed tears and fought hard. She cried and begged to be allowed to go to school but all the begging was on deaf ears.

As the church meeting was coming to an end, Edith was happy that she had survived the forced marriage arrangements. She was an intelligent child always coming first in her class. She had escaped to her uncle's house trying to evade the church camp meeting but the plan did not work as her father demanded that she comes home without wasting time.

As the people were folding the tents and preparing to leave, Edith was called by her father with the mother joining her.

"Edith you are a beautiful girl and I don't doubt that you are going to be a great wife, always listening to your husband and no talking back. You will do all that he asks you to do."

Edith smiled and responded, "Yes, mom one day when I finish school I will meet someone I love and get married and start a family.

"You do not have to wait for all that long, my daughter," the mother interjected. "We have already found a man for you and look at him, he has fields, businesses and he will be taking care of you."

A man in his late forties was approaching the parents. He cleared his throat to announce his arrival. "Good evening brothers and sister in the lord. I hope I am not interrupting an important conversation?" he asked.

There was an awkward silence revealing that there was unfinished business. He figured out that there was a discussion to hand over the girl that he had been promised when the parents had failed to repay a debt of USD 200 that the parents had borrowed over time. They had hoped that they were going to be paid for the work the husband had done for someone but that did not materialize.

The creditor ran out of patience. He stepped forward and grabbed Edith like a shepherd carrying kid. Edith wriggled and screamed as she was taken away but that did not help, the parents had mixed emotions. They really wanted their daughter to finish school but it was too late, the agreement they made could not be reversed. And so it was.

The following morning Edith's father, Samson Mabwe, went to a man he had done work for and managed to get USD 220 after narrating the story but when they visited Murindagomo, the man they had offered Edith as settlement of debt with a proposal to recover their child and settle the amount, the man refused to budge stating that Edith was very intelligent and he needed her to run his businesses. Murindagomo had sent Edith to a boarding school after her plea to finish school. The man however refused to let them know where Edith was, stating that she was his wife and he had a right to send her anywhere he wished and would not be pushed to disclose what he was doing with his wives at his homestead.

On the other hand Noel took the girl he had "Prophesied" about. They all drove home in silence in the family minivan. Then they got home, Noel's wives did what was once done to them. They tied Natasha's hands and legs and sent her into one of the bedrooms. They gave her a lecture about being intimate with a man and how difficult life was going to be at her newly found home.

An hour later dinner was brought but Natasha refused to eat. At midnight Noel entered the bedroom and unbound Natasha. He was holding a glass of Amarula and a cigarette of marijuana.

"You smoke?" Natasha asked. Noel did not take kindly any questioning but he decided to move with the flow.

"Yes, I drink and I smoke too," Noel said. Natasha looked at him. She moved closer to him to dispel the notion that she wanted to run away.

"Can we drink together and possibly smoke together?"

Noel looked at her and had to admit that she was intelligent. He looked at her then walked to the kitchen to take another glass much to the surprise of the other wives who were eagerly waiting to know how and when he was going to violate the new girl as he had done to them.

That night Natasha and Noel drank Amarula and almost at 4 am, there were screams coming from Natasha's bedroom, Noel had turned into an animal as he did with other girls when he brought them. He repeatedly raped her. She cried for help, she wanted out, she wanted to go but nobody could hear her. This went on for days and into weeks till she got used to it and till she was totally brain washed and was filled with the rage.

Just after her 14th birthday she discovered that she was pregnant and that's when she became suicidal and hatched a plan to destroy Noel. Destroy the whole family, blot out Noel's name and anything that was related to him.

Want to keep reading?
The gods Above is available now in paperback and e-book.
Search for **Elliot Chatima and Rumbi Chen** on Amazon or your favourite online bookstore to get your copy today!